P9-DFF-396

Dear Reader,

From February 2013 onward, Harlequin Romance will continue to offer four great reads every month, with all the themes you love, such as babies, weddings, bosses, pregnancies and more.

You can also find some of the authors you have come to know and love from Harlequin Romance in our new contemporary series Harlequin KISS, which is launching in February 2013.

Happy reading!

The Harlequin Romance Editors

P.S. Available this month:

#4357 THE HEIR'S PROPOSAL
Raye Morgan

#4358 THE SOLDIER'S SWEETHEART
The Larkville Legacy
Soraya Lane

#4359 THE BILLIONAIRE'S FAIR LADY
Barbara Wallace

#4360 A BRIDE FOR THE MAVERICK MILLIONAIRE
Journey Through the Outback
Marion Lennox

#4361 SHIPWRECKED WITH MR. WRONG
Nikki Logan

#4362 WHEN CHOCOLATE IS NOT ENOUGH...
Nina Harrington

"Mommy's back!" Steffi jumped from her seat and ran toward the door. Mike followed behind. At this point he wasn't sure who was happier to see them return. That is, he was eager to see how his investment paid off.

The main office door opened and—*wow!* Mike had to grab hold of the reception desk to keep his balance. The woman walking through the door with Sophie was... Was...

He'd lost his ability to speak. Her red mane had been tamed into thick strawberry plaits that tumbled about her shoulders. The skinny jeans and sweater were gone. Tossed in favor of a black-and-white wraparound dress and cardigan sweater that subtly showed off her curves. The hint of flesh dipping to a V between her breasts was as enticing as any low-cut camisole. And her legs... Discreetly, he stole a look at her bottom half.

Her eyes found his, looking for his reaction. Had her skin always looked this luminescent or was it the expertly applied makeup?

"You look amazing," he replied.

"Then I guess the transformation is complete."

A shadow flickered across her face....

BARBARA WALLACE

The Billionaire's Fair Lady

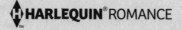
HARLEQUIN® ROMANCE

If you purchased this book without a cover you should be aware
that this book is stolen property. It was reported as "unsold and
destroyed" to the publisher, and neither the author nor the
publisher has received any payment for this "stripped book."

Recycling programs
for this product may
not exist in your area.

ISBN-13: 978-0-373-74224-0

THE BILLIONAIRE'S FAIR LADY

First North American Publication 2013

Copyright © 2013 by Barbara Wallace

All rights reserved. Except for use in any review, the reproduction or
utilization of this work in whole or in part in any form by any electronic,
mechanical or other means, now known or hereafter invented, including
xerography, photocopying and recording, or in any information storage
or retrieval system, is forbidden without the written permission of the
publisher, Harlequin Enterprises Limited, 225 Duncan Mill Road,
Don Mills, Ontario M3B 3K9, Canada.

This is a work of fiction. Names, characters, places and incidents are
either the product of the author's imagination or are used fictitiously,
and any resemblance to actual persons, living or dead, business
establishments, events or locales is entirely coincidental.

This edition published by arrangement with Harlequin Books S.A.

For questions and comments about the quality of this book,
please contact us at CustomerService@Harlequin.com.

® and TM are trademarks of Harlequin Enterprises Limited or its
corporate affiliates. Trademarks indicated with ® are registered in the
United States Patent and Trademark Office, the Canadian Trade Marks
Office and in other countries.

HARLEQUIN®

Printed in U.S.A.

www.Harlequin.com

Barbara Wallace is a lifelong romantic and daydreamer, so it's not surprising that at the age of eight she decided to become a writer. However, it wasn't until a coworker handed her a romance novel that she knew where her stories belonged. For years she limited her dreams to nights, weekends and commuter train trips, while working as a communications specialist, PR freelancer and full-time mom. At the urging of her family, she finally chucked the day job and pursued writing full-time—and she couldn't be happier.

Barbara lives in Massachusetts with her husband, their teenage son and two very spoiled, self-centred cats (as if there could be any other kind). Readers can visit her at www.barbarawallace.com and find her on Facebook. She'd love to hear from you.

Books by Barbara Wallace

MR. RIGHT, NEXT DOOR!
DARING TO DATE THE BOSS
A FAIRYTALE CHRISTMAS*
THE CINDERELLA BRIDE
THE HEART OF A HERO
BEAUTY AND THE BROODING BOSS

*Anthology with Susan Meier

Other titles by this author available in ebook format.

To the fabulous Donna Alward, who talked me off ledges and pushed me to get this story on paper. You're the best!

To Flo, the best editor a woman could ask for.

To the real Fran and Alice for providing the legal background information. Thanks for the help.

And, as always, to my boys Pete and Andrew, who put up with an awful lot so I can live my dream of writing stories for a living.

CHAPTER ONE

HE DIDN'T believe her.

Color her not surprised. *You've got to go up-town to fight uptown.* Minute the thought entered her brain, she should have shoved it aside. After all, bad ideas were a Roxy O'Brien specialty. But no, she opened the phone directory and picked the first uptown law firm whose ad mentioned wills. Which was why she now sat in her best imitation business outfit—really her waitress uniform with a new plaid blazer—waiting for Michael Temple-ton, attorney at law, to deliver his verdict.

"Where did you say you found these letters?" he asked. His gold-rimmed reading glasses couldn't mask the skeptical glint in his brown eyes. "Your mother's closet?"

"Yes," she replied. "In a shoe box." Tucked under a collection of seasonal sweaters.

"And you didn't know they existed before then?"

"I didn't know anything until last month."

That was putting it mildly. Her head was still reeling.

The attorney didn't reply. Again, not surprising. He'd done very little talking the entire meeting. In fact, Roxy got the distinct impression he found the whole appointment something of a trial. Something to get through so he could move on to more important, more believable business.

To his credit, disbelief or not, he didn't rush her out the door. He let her lay out her story without interruption, and was now carefully reading the letter in his hand. The first of what was a collection of thirty, all lovingly preserved in chronological order. Her mother's secret.

You have his eyes.

The memory rolled through her. Four words. Fourteen letters. With the power to change her life. One minute she was Roxanne O'Brien, daughter of Fiona and Connor O'Brien, the next she was… Who? The daughter of some man she'd never met. A lover her mother never—ever—mentioned. That's why she came to Mike Templeton. To find answers.

Well, maybe a little bit more than answers. After all, if her mother told the truth, then she, Roxy O'Brien whoever, could be entitled to a far different life. A far better life.

You have his eyes.

Speaking of eyes, Mike Templeton had set down the letter and sat studying her. Roxy'd been stared at before. Customers figured ogling the waitress came with the bar tab. And they were the polite ones. So she'd grown immune to looks long ago. Or so she'd thought. For some reason, Mike Templeton's stare made her want to squirm. Maybe because he'd removed his glasses, giving her an unobstructed view of what were really very intense brown eyes. It felt like he wasn't so much looking at her as trying to see inside. Read her mind, or gauge her intentions. A self-conscious flutter found its way to her stomach. She recrossed her legs, wishing her skirt wasn't so damn short, and forced herself to maintain eye contact. A visual Mexican standoff.

To her relief, he broke first, sitting back in his leather chair. Roxy found her eyes drawn to the black lacquered pen he twirled between his long, elegant fingers.

Everything about him was elegant, she thought to herself. His fingers, his "bearing" as her high school drama teacher would say. He fit the surroundings, that's for sure, right down to the tailored suit and crisp white shirt. Roxy wasn't sure, but she thought she'd seen a similar look on the pages of a men's fashion magazine. Simply sitting across from him made her feel every inch the downtown girl.

Except, if what her mother said was true, she wasn't so downtown after all, was she?"

"Are all the letters this…intimate?" he asked.

Cheeks warming, Roxy nodded. "I think so. I skimmed most of them." Like the man said, the letters were intimate. Reading them closely felt too much like reading a stranger's diary.

A stranger who was her father. Come to think of it, the woman described on those pages didn't sound very much like her mother, either.

"You'll notice the dates, though," she told him. "The last letter is postmarked. Nine months before I was born."

"As well as a couple of weeks before his accident."

The car accident that killed him. Roxy had read a brief account when doing her internet research.

The attorney frowned. Somehow he managed to make even that expression look sophisticated. "You're positive your mother never said anything before last month?"

He was kidding, right? Roxy shot him a long look. What was with all these repetitive questions anyway? She'd already laid out her whole story. If he planned on dismissing her, then dismiss her.

Why waste time? "I think I would have remembered if she did."

"And she didn't explain why?"

"Unfortunately she was too busy dying."

The words were out before Roxy could pull them back, causing the lawyer's eyebrows to arch. Clearly not the best way to impress the man.

Seriously though, how did he expect her to answer? That while on her deathbed, her mother laid out a detailed and concise explanation of her affair with Wentworth Sinclair? "She was pretty out of things," Roxy said, doing her best to choke back the sarcasm. "At first I thought it was the painkillers talking." Until her mother's eyes had cleared for that one, brief instant. *You have his eyes...*

"Now you think otherwise."

"Based on what I read in those letters, yes."

"Hmmm."

That was it. Just hmmm. He'd begun twirling the pen again. Roxy didn't like the silence. Reminded her too much of the expectant pause that followed an audition speech while the casting director made notes. Here the expectation felt even thicker. Probably because the stakes were so much higher.

"So let me see if I have this straight," he said finally, drawing out his words. "Your mother just happens to tell you on her deathbed that you're the daughter of Wentworth Sinclair, the dead son of one of New York's wealthiest families. Then, when cleaning out her belongings, you just happen to find a stack of love letters that not only corroborates your claim, but lays out a timeline that ends right before his death." He gave the pen another couple of twirls. "Ties up pretty conveniently, wouldn't you say? The fact both parties are dead and unable to dispute your story?"

"Why would they dispute anything? I'm telling the truth." Roxy didn't like where this conversation was heading one little bit. "If you're suggesting I'm making the story up—" She *knew* he didn't believe her.

"I'm not suggesting anything. I'm simply pointing out the facts, which are convenient." He leaned forward, fingers folded in front of him. "Do you know how many people claim to be long-lost heirs?"

"No." Nor did she care about any claim but hers, which happened to be true.

"More than you'd realize. Just last week, for example, a man came in saying he'd traced his family tree back to Henry Hudson. He wanted to know if he was eligible for reparation from the city of New York for his share of the Hudson River."

"And your point?" Anger ticking upward, she gritted her teeth.

"My point," he replied, leaning closer, "is that he had more paperwork than you."

Son of a— The man all but called her a fraud. No, worse. He was implying she made up the story like it was some kind of scam. As if she hadn't spent the past month questioning everything she'd known about her life. How dare he? "You think I'm lying about being Wentworth Sinclair's daughter?"

"People have done more for less."

"I— You—" It took every ounce of restraint not to grab the nameplate off his desk and smash it over his head. "This isn't about money," she spat at him.

"Really?" He sat back. "So you have no interest at all in gaining a share of the Sinclair millions?"

Roxy opened her mouth, then shut it. She'd like nothing better than to say absolutely not and make him feel like a condescending heel, but they both knew she'd be lying. If it were only her, or if she lived in a perfect world, she could afford to be virtuous, but it wasn't only about her. And Lord knows her world was far from perfect. That was the point. Being Wentworth Sinclair's daughter could be her only shot at not screwing up the one worthwhile thing in her miserable life.

Try explaining that to someone like Mike Templeton, however. What would he know about mistakes and imperfect worlds? He'd probably spent his whole life watching everything he'd touched turn to gold.

Right now, he was smirking at her reaction. "That's what I thought. Sorry, but if you're looking for a payout, you'll have to do better than a stack of thirty-year-old love letters."

"Twenty-nine," Roxy corrected, although really, why bother? He'd already made up his mind she was some lying money-grabber.

"Twenty-nine then. Either way, next time I suggest you try bringing a document that's more useful, like a birth certificate perhaps."

"You mean the one naming Wentworth Sinclair as my father?" The battle against sarcasm failed, badly, and she mockingly slapped her forehead. "Silly me, I left it at home." When he gave her a pointed look, she returned it with an equally pointed expression of her own. He wasn't the only one who could do judgmental. "Don't you think if I had something like that, I would have brought it with me?"

"One would think, but then one would think your mother would have named the correct father thirty years ago, too." He was folding the letter and placing it back in its envelope. Roxy wanted to grab his long fingers and squeeze them until he yelped. One would think. Maybe her mother had been afraid no one would believe her either.

"You know what," she said, reaching for the stack of letters, "forget this."

What made her think uptown would want to help her? Uptown didn't care about people like her, period, and she'd be damned if she was going to sit here and let some stuffed-shirt lawyer look down his nose at her. "The only reason I came here was that your directory ad said you handled wills and estates, and I *thought* you could help me. Apparently I was wrong."

She snatched her leather coat off the back of her chair. If Mike Templeton didn't think her problems were worth his time, then he wasn't worth hers. "I'm sure another law firm will be willing to listen."

"Miss O'Brien, I think you misunderstood. Please sit down."

No, Roxy didn't feel like sitting down. Or listening to any kind of explanation. Why? Rejection was rejection regardless of how many pretty words you attached to it. She should know. She'd heard enough "thanks but no thanks" in her lifetime. And they felt like kicks to the stomach.

She jammed her arm into her coat sleeve. Emotion clogged her throat, and she absolutely refused to let him see her eyes water.

"By the way," she said, adjusting her collar. "Your ad said you welcomed all types of cases. If you don't mean it, then don't say so in the headline."

An unnecessary jab, but she was tired of playing polite and classy. Besides, being called a gold-digging fraud should entitle her to at least one parting shot.

"Miss O'Brien—"

She strode from the office without turning around, proud that she got as far as street level before her vision grew blurry.

Dammit. She'd have thought she'd be cried out by now. When would she stop feeling so raw and exposed?

You have his eyes...

"Why didn't you say anything, Mom?" she railed silently. "Why did you wait till it was too late to tell me?"

Was she that ashamed of her daughter?

Not cool, Templeton, Not cool at all.

Mike had to admit, though, as indignant exits went, Roxy O'Brien's was among the best. Ten years of estate law had shown him his share of scam artists and gold diggers, but she was the first who'd truly teared up upon storming out. She probably didn't think he noticed, but he had. There was no mistaking the overly bright sheen in those green eyes of hers, in spite of her attempts to blink them dry.

Pen twirling between his fingers, he rocked back and forth in his chair. Couldn't blame her for being upset. Like a lot of people, she must have thought she'd stumbled across the legal equivalent of a winning lottery ticket. If she'd stuck around instead of stomping off like a redheaded windstorm he'd have explained that making a claim against the Sinclairs wasn't that simple, even if her story was true. There were legal precedents and statutes of limitations to consider.

Of course, he thought, stilling his pen, she didn't have to completely prove paternity for her claim to work. Simply put forth a believable argument.

He couldn't believe he was contemplating the thought. Had he fallen so low he'd take on an audacious case simply for the potential settlement money?

One look at the meager pile of case files on his desk answered his question. At this point, he'd take Henry Hudson's nephew's case.

This was what failure felt like. The constant hollow feeling in his stomach. The weight on his shoulders. The tick, tick, tick in the back of his head reminding him another day was passing without clients knocking on his door.

It wasn't supposed to be like this. Templetons, as had been drilled in his head, didn't fail. They blazed trails. They excelled. They were leaders in their field. Doubly so if you were named Michael Templeton III and had two generations of name-sakes to live up to.

You're letting us down, Michael. We raised you to be better than this. A dozen years after he first heard them, his father's words rose up to repeat themselves, reminding him he had no choice. Succeed or else. He took on the challenge of starting his own practice. He had to make it work, by hook or by crook.

Or audacious case, as it were. Unfortunately his best opportunity stormed out the door in a huff. So how did he get the little hothead to come back?

A patch of gray caught the corner of his eye. Realizing what he was looking at, Mike smiled. Perhaps his luck hadn't run out after all. He picked up the grey envelope Roxanne O'Brien had left behind.

God bless indignant exits.

Thursday nights were always busy at the Elderion Lounge. The customers, businessmen mostly, their out-of-town visits winding down, tended to cut loose. Bar tabs got bigger, rounds more frequent, tables more boisterous. Normally Roxy didn't mind the extra action since it meant more money in her pocket. Tonight, though, she wasn't in the mood for salesmen knocking back vodka tonics.

"Six vodka tonics, one house pinot and two pom martinis," she ordered. Despite being cold outside, the air was stifling and hot. She grabbed a cocktail napkin and blotted her neckline. This afternoon's business jacket disappeared long ago and she was back to a black camisole and skirt.

The bartender, a beefy guy named Dion, looked her up and down. "You look frazzled. Table six isn't giving you trouble, are they?"

"Nothing I can't handle. Bad day is all."

Who did Mike Templeton think he was anyway? Arrogant, condescending… Just because he was lucky enough to be born on the right side of town, what made him think he had the right to judge her or her mother or anyone else for that matter?

Wadding the napkin into a ball, she tossed it neatly into the basket behind the bar. "You'd think by this point I'd be immune to rejection."

"I thought you gave up acting," Dion said.

"I did. This was something else." And the rejection stung worse. "You don't know a good lawyer, do you?"

The bartender immediately frowned. "You in trouble?"

"Nothing like that. I need a business lawyer."

"Oh." He shook his head. "Sorry."

"'S'all right." Who's to say the next guy wouldn't be as condescending as Mike Templeton?

"Oh, my God!" Jackie, one of the other waitresses rushed up, earrings and bangle bracelets jangling. "Please let this guy sit at my table."

Busy stacking her tray, Roxy didn't bother looking up. At least once a week, the man of Jackie's dreams walked in. "What's the deal this time? He look like someone famous?"

"Try rich."

Here? Hardly. Unless the guy was lost and needed directions. Rich men hung at far better clubs. "I suppose he's gorgeous, too."

"Put it this way. If he was poor, I'd still make a move. He's that sexy."

Roxy had to see this male specimen for herself. Craning her neck, she surveyed the crowd. "I seriously doubt anyone with that much to offer—"

Mike Templeton stood by table eight, peeling the gloves off his hands one finger at a time. His eyes scanned the room with a heavy-lidded scrutiny. Roxy's stomach dropped. Jackie was right, he was the best-looking man in the room. Stood out like a pro in a field of amateurs. What on earth was he doing here?

"Told you he was breathtaking," she heard

Jackie say. Before she could reply, he turned and their eyes locked. She stood rooted to the spot as he shrugged off his camel hair coat and draped it over the back of his chair. His actions were slow, deliberate, all the while holding her gaze. Goose bumps danced up her bare arms. It felt like she was the one removing layers.

"I don't suppose I can convince you to switch tables, can I? You're not interested in dating anyway. I'll give you both my twelve and fifteen."

Eyes still glued to the lawyer, Roxy shook her head. "Sorry, Jackie, no can do. Not this time."

Grabbing her tray, she purposely served her other tables before making her way toward him. With her back to that stare, his pull diminished a little, though she could still feel him watching her with every move she made. Reminding her of his existence. As if she could forget.

Finally she had no choice—or customers—left and sauntered her way to his table.

"You're a difficult person to pin down, Miss O'Brien," he greeted. "I went by your apartment first and some guy told me you were 'at the bar.' I took a chance and assumed he meant here." He smiled, as though being there was the most natural thing in the world, which it was decidedly not. "We never finished our conversation from earlier."

The guy had to be joking. "What was there to

finish? I pretty much heard everything I needed to hear when you insulted me and my mother."

"You misunderstood. I wasn't trying to insult you. Had you stuck around, you would have realized I was merely pointing out your story has some very questionable holes in it."

"My mistake." Misunderstood her foot. If that was his idea of a misunderstanding, then she was the Queen of New York. "Next time my life is turned upside down by a deathbed confession, I'll try to make sure the story is more complete."

She tucked her tray under her arm. "Is there anything else? I've got customers to wait on." He wasn't the only one who could be dismissive.

"I'll have a Scotch. Neat."

Great. He planned to stick around. Maybe she would let Jackie have the table. "Anything else?"

"Yes, there is. You forgot this." Reaching into his briefcase, he pulled out a gray envelope. Seeing it, Roxy nearly groaned out loud. "Your mother took so much effort to preserve the collection. Seemed a shame to break up the set."

She felt like an idiot. Figures she'd mess up her grand exit. She never was good at stage directions. "Thank you. But you didn't have to drive all the way here to return it. You could have mailed it back to me."

"No problem at all. I didn't want to risk the envelope being damaged. Besides…"

Roxy had been reaching for the stack, when his hand came down to cover hers. "I figured this would buy me a few more minutes of your time," he finished, his eyes catching hers.

Warmth spread through Roxy's body, starting with her arm and moving upward. Glancing down at the table, she saw his hand still covered hers. The tapered fingers were almost twice the size of hers. If he wanted, he would wrap her hand right up in a strong, tight embrace. Feeling the warmth seeping into her cheeks, she pulled free.

"For what?" she asked, gripping her tray tightly. Squeezing the hard plastic helped chase away the sensation his hand left behind.

"I told you. You left before we could finish our conversation."

"Given what I stuck around for, can you blame me? I'll go get your drink."

"Tsk, tsk, tsk," he said as soon as she'd spun around. "You're going to need a lot thicker skin than that if you want to go after the Sinclairs."

Roxy froze. What did he say?

"That is why you came by to see me, isn't it?" he continued. "Because you want to make a claim against Wentworth Sinclair's estate?"

She was afraid to say yes, in case the other shoe

dropped on her head. Slowly she turned around to find the lawyer looking more than a little pleased with himself for having caught her off guard. Was he trying to tell her she had a case after all?

So help him, if he was playing with her....

"Look, here's the deal." He leaned forward, gold cuff links catching the light. "Your case is a long shot. Both parties have passed away, and the only proof you have is a pile of love letters. Not to mention thirty years have gone by. The courts aren't exactly generous when it comes to claims that old. Truth is, scaling Mount Everest would be easier."

"Thanks for the recap." And here she thought there was something to his comment. "If that's what you came all the way over here to tell me, you wasted the gas."

"You're not letting me finish again."

Roxy stopped. Although hearing him out seemed like a waste of time to her. How many times did she need to hear him say her case wasn't good enough for him? "Okay," she said, waiting. "Finish. My case is harder than climbing Mount Everest. What else do you need to tell me?"

A slow smile broke out across his face. A confident smile that stilled everything in her body. "Only that I happen to really enjoy mountain climbing."

CHAPTER TWO

"I'LL, um, go get your drink." Spinning around, Roxy made a beeline to the bar. It was the only response she could think of. Did he say what she thought he said? He was taking her case?

"You look like a truck hit you," Jackie remarked when she reached the bar rail. "What happened? Richie Rich turn out to be a creep?"

If she weren't still in a daze, Roxy would comment on the hopeful expectancy in the other woman's voice. "Not a creep. My lawyer," she corrected.

"I thought you said you didn't have one," Dion said.

"I didn't think I did." She still wasn't sure. She didn't trust her ears. For that matter, she wasn't entirely sure she trusted Mike Templeton. There had to be a catch.

Quickly she looked over her shoulder. There he sat, stiff and formal, arranging what looked like paperwork on the table. He certainly didn't seem the type to lead someone on.

"If you're serious," she said, when her rounds finally brought him back to his table, "then what was all that business about Henry Hudson and not having proof?"

"Had to figure out how loyal you were to your story somehow, didn't I?" he remarked, raising the glass to his lips.

"Un-freaking-believable." It was a *test*. If it weren't such an amazingly bad idea, she'd pour Scotch in his lap. She still might. "Do you have any idea how pis— How upset I was?"

"From the way you stormed out, I could hazard a guess. But that also tipped the scale in your favor. Either you truly believed your story or you were a damn good actress."

She could give him a long list of directors and casting agents who could refute the latter. Still, a *test?* She had half a mind to tell him he could stuff himself regardless of whether he wanted to take on her claim or not. "I can't believe you. Are you like this with everyone who tries to hire you?"

"Only the ones claiming to be heirs to multi-million-dollar fortunes."

Millions? Was he joking? Roxy checked his expression. His face was deadly serious.

Oh, my. She dropped into the seat across from him. "Millions?" she repeated.

"What were you expecting?"

"I don't know." She swiped the hair from her face, trying to focus. "I knew they were rich, but... Wow."

His test was beginning to make a bit of sense. Millions. A tingle ran up her spine.

"There's no guarantee, mind you. Like I said, the courts seldom rule in favor of claims like yours."

Mind still reeling, Roxy nodded.

"Plus, the Sinclairs' lawyers will put up a heck of a fight. This isn't the first time someone's challenged their estate, I'm sure. Nevertheless, if we play our cards right, and there's no reason to believe I won't, we'll both be looking at a nice little payday."

Again, Roxy nodded. She didn't know what else to do. His proclamation had stunned her to silence.

"Yo, Roxy! Table four!" Dion called. "Get your butt in gear."

A few feet away, a trio of women with empty martini glasses were looking in her direction, visibly annoyed.

"You better get to your customers," Mike noted.

He watched with amusement as the waitress half stumbled, half rushed away. Funny how her expression went from annoyed to dazed in literally the blink of an eye. The prospect of money could do that to a person. Made him jump in his car and drive to this place, didn't it?

For a moment he'd been afraid he'd laid it on a little too heavy with that "test" stuff, but she accepted his behavior. All he needed to do now was get her to cooperate with the rest of the case. Shouldn't be too hard. Especially given her alternative.

Leaning back in his chair, he sipped his drink and looked around the bar. As bars went, the Elderion was in the upper-lower half. Below average, but far enough up to avoid being a dive. Both the tables and the clientele had mileage.

Wentworth's letter lay where Roxanne dropped it. He ran his finger along the edge of the gray envelope. The contents had long been committed to memory. *"I can still smell your scent on my skin,"* Wentworth had written for the opening line. College passion. He knew it well. That heady reckless feeling. The blind confidence the days would last forever. Until reality barged in with its expectations and traditions waiting to be fulfilled and impractical dreams had to be shoved aside.

Look at you. We raised you to be better than this, Michael.

A hollow feeling lodged in his stomach. He

blamed the surroundings. Ever since walking in to the Elderion, he'd been possessed by the strangest feeling of déjà vu. Memories of another bar with dim lights and warm beer came floating back. When quality and atmosphere took a backseat to political debates and slow dancing in the dark.

His semester of ill-spent youth. He hadn't thought about those days in years. They'd been jettisoned to the past when he took his first law internship.

A few feet away, his new client—least he hoped she was his new client—negotiated her way through the narrow tables with the grace of a dancer. Amazing she could navigate anything in that scrap of cloth she called a uniform. Without the pink-and-gray blazer for coverage, he had a perfect view of how the spandex skirt molded to her curves. An open invitation to check out the assets. As she bent over, the skirt pulled tighter. Forget invitation, Mike decided, try full-blown neon sign. Feeling an uncomfortable tightness, he shifted his legs. Definitely not what his usual client would wear.

But then, this case wasn't his usual case. In fact, it was everything he'd been taught to avoid— splashy, risky, generating more notoriety than respect. Beggars couldn't be choosers could they? Beat closing his doors and telling his family he wasn't the Templeton they'd groomed him to be. Watching Roxanne dodge the palm of a customer right before it caressed her bottom, he retrieved his pen and made a quick note: smooth out the rough edges.

It was an hour later before Roxanne returned to his table, carrying with her a bottle of water. Mike tried not to stare at her legs as she approached. Given her outfit, it was a Herculean task at best. "You're still here," she said.

"Seemed silly to drive all the way back to the office when I could work here." He'd stacked what little legal work he did have in piles on the desk.

"It's eight o'clock. Most people have stopped working by now."

"Maybe in this place, but I'm not most people." He should know. It'd been drilled into his head enough growing up. "I also figured you'd have questions."

"You're right. I do." She pointed to the empty chair. "Do you mind?"

"Your big bad boss won't care?"

"I'm on my ten."

"Then be my guest. What's your question?"

"Well, first…" She picked at the label on her water bottle, obviously searching for the right words. "Are you sure you weren't kidding? About it being a million-dollar claim? That wasn't another one of your tests, was it?"

Ah, straight to the money. "I told you, I don't kid. Not about case value. Although keep in mind, I'm not making any promises, either. I'm saying there's potential. Nothing more."

"I appreciate the honesty. I don't like being misled."

"Me, neither," he replied. Seemed the hothead had a bit of a cautious streak after all. A good sign.

He watched as she peeled off a strip of label. "So what's the next step?" she asked. "Do I take a DNA test or something?"

If it were so easy. "Easy there, Cowboy. Don't get ahead of yourself. It's a little more complicated. You got any Sinclair DNA lying around?" he asked her.

Immediately her eyes went to the envelope. Cautious *and* quick. "I'm afraid you've watched too many crime shows. Getting anything off letters that old would be a miracle." Besides, he'd already had a similar thought and checked online. "You're going to need a more recent sample."

"How do we get one?"

Now they were getting to the complicated part. "Best way would be for one of the Sinclair sisters to agree to a test. They are Wentworth's closest living relatives."

"But you said they would put up a fight."

"Doesn't mean we don't ask," he told her. "We give them enough evidence, and they'll have to comply."

"You mean, prove I'm a Sinclair, and they'll let me have proof."

Mike couldn't help smiling. Definitely quick. He liked that. If he had to take a case like this, he preferred to work with a client who understood what they were doing. Made his job easier. "Never fear. We'll make enough noise that they'll have to pay attention. The squeaky wheel and that sort of thing."

Frowning, she tore another strip. Some of the eagerness had left her face. Without it, she looked tired and, dare he say, a bit vulnerable. "You make it sound like I'm out to get them."

"The Sinclairs would argue you are."

"Why? I didn't go looking for this. My mother dropped the story in my lap."

"A story you promptly took to a lawyer to see if you have a claim to his estate."

That silenced her. "I didn't look at it that way." Another strip peeled away. "I'm just trying to make my life better. If this guy—Wentworth Sinclair—was my father, he'd want that, too, wouldn't he?"

Mike had to admit, if the relationship painted

in the letter he read carried forward, she might be right. "Which is why we're pursuing the claim. To help you get that better life."

"What if they refuse to listen?"

"Then we'll keep fighting," Mike answered simply. Sooner or later, the Sinclairs would have to pay attention if only to make them disappear. He wasn't kidding about the squeaky wheel; it always yielded some kind of result.

Roxy was looking down at the table. Following her gaze, Mike saw that at some point while talking, he'd once again covered her hand. When had he reached across? When the dimness hit her eyes? That wasn't like him. He always kept an invisible wall between himself and his clients. For good reason. Getting too close led to making mistakes.

He studied the hand beneath his. She had skin the color of eggshells, pale and off-white. There was a small tattoo on the inside of her wrist as well. A yellow butterfly. The wings called out for a thumb to brush across them.

Mike realized he was about to do just that when she pulled her hand free and balled it into a fist. He found himself doing the same.

"Why?" she asked aloud.

Distracted by his reaction to the butterfly, it took a moment for her question to register. "Why what?"

"Why would you fight for me? If it's such a long shot, why are you taking this case?"

Somehow he didn't think she'd appreciate the truth, that he needed the money from this case as badly as she wanted it. "Told you, I like a challenge. As for fighting, I don't believe in quitting. Or losing. So you can be assured, I'll stick around to the bloody end."

"Colorful term."

"I also don't believe in mincing words."

"That so? Never would have guessed from your gentle desk side manner." She smiled as she delivered the comment. Mike fought the urge to smile back, taking a sip of his drink instead.

"You can have hand-holding or you can have results." Unfortunate choice of words given his behavior a moment earlier. "Up to you."

"Results are fine," she replied. "In my book, hand-holding is overrated. Sympathy just leads to a whole lot of unwanted problems."

Add practical to her list of attributes. Maybe this case would go smoother than he thought, in spite of this morning's dramatics. "I agree."

"Still…"

Mike's senses went on alert. Any sentence beginning with the word "still" never ended well. "What is it?"

"Don't get me wrong. I'm not looking for reassurance, but I'm wondering. When you say the word bloody, just how bloody do you mean?"

"The Sinclair legal team won't hold back, if that's what you're asking. They'll have no qualms about digging into your life." Her expression fell, followed quickly by his stomach. She had a skeleton, didn't she? "If you've got secrets, you best start sharing."

"No secrets." She shook her head, a little too vehemently if you asked him.

"Then what?"

"I've got a kid. A little girl. Her name is Steffi."

Wentworth Sinclair's granddaughter. That wasn't what he expected to hear. "No problem," he replied. His enthusiasm started building. Alice and Frances Sinclair would no doubt be very interested in the little girl's existence. "In fact, this might actually make the case—"

"Whoa!" She held up her hand, cutting him off. "I don't want her involved. She's only four years old. She won't understand what's going on."

Mike took a deep breath. "I don't think you understand. The fact that Wentworth might have a granddaughter could go a long way in convincing the sisters to comply with our requests."

She shook her head. "I don't care. I'm not going to have her being upset. She can't be involved. You'll have to find a different way."

"I don't think—"

"Promise."

What was he going to do? He wanted to tell her she was in no position to issue conditions, that as her lawyer, it was his job to do everything he could to win her case, meaning he was the one who would decide what tactics he could or couldn't use. He also wanted to tell her there was no way he could keep such a promise. Sooner or later the Sinclair sisters would discover the child's existence. Her fiercely determined expression stopped him from saying so. There was no way he'd get her to budge on the issue tonight. Push and he ran the risk of her walking away again.

"Fine." He'd agree to her condition for now, and renegotiate their position later.

"Thank you." Satisfied, she opened her now naked water bottle and took a long drink. "When do we start?"

The spark had returned to her eyes, turning them brilliantly green. She was leaning forward, too, enough to remind him her tank top was extremely low cut. His legal mind definitely did not appreciate the male awareness the sight caused. Definitely had to smooth out the rough edges.

"Soon," he told her. "Very soon."

He stayed the rest of the evening. Nursing his drink and scribbling notes on his yellow legal pad.

Damn unnerving it was, too. His existence filled the entire room making it impossible to ignore him. Three times she messed up an order because he distracted her, mistakes Dion made clear he planned to take out of her check.

Why was he sticking around anyway? He'd returned her letter, they'd talked. Shouldn't he be at his uptown apartment, drinking expensive Scotch by a fireplace? Surely he wasn't sticking around for the ambience. No one came to the Elderion for the ambiance.

"Maybe he wants to negotiate payment," Jackie teased. Ever since Roxy had mentioned the fact Mike was working on a legal problem for her the other waitress wouldn't stop with the innuendos.

"Very funny," she shot back, though the comment did make her hair stand on edge. They hadn't talked about payment. How did he expect her to pay for his services?

His presence continued to dog her as she delivered a round to the table next to his. Thank goodness the patrons all ordered bottled beer. She wasn't sure she could handle anything more complicated while standing in such close proximity.

Funny thing was the guy hadn't looked in her direction. Not once, and she'd been checking fairly frequently. Staring she could handle. She got looks every night. So why couldn't she shake Mike Templeton? Why did she feel that same penetrating scrutiny she felt back at his office every time she walked in his line of sight? All night long, it felt like he was right behind her, staring at her soul.

Another thing. He insisted on looking good. By this point in the night, the rest of the men in the place had long shed their jackets and ties. Heck, some were close to shedding their shirts. The room smelled of damp skin and aftershave.

Mike, however, barely looked bothered. His tie remained tightly knotted, and he still wore his suit jacket. Roxy didn't even think there were wrinkles in his shirt. If he was going to stick around, the least he could do was try to blend in with the rest of the drunken businessmen.

"Why are you still here?" she finally asked, when her rounds brought her to his table.

He looked up from the chicken scratches he'd been making on his notepad. "I'd like to think the answer's apparent. I'm working."

"I can see that. Why are you still working?"

She expected him to say something equally obvious such as "I'm not done yet" but he didn't. Instead he got an unusually faraway look in his eye. "I have to."

No, Roxy thought. *She* had to. A guy like Mike Templeton chose to. In the interest of good relations, she kept the difference to herself, and instead tried to decipher the notes in front of her. "Smooth out the rough edges? What does that mean?"

"Part of my overall strategy. I'm still fleshing it out."

"You planning to share it with me?"

"Eventually." The vague answer didn't sit well. Too much like information being kept from her, and she'd had enough of that this month. "Why can't I see now?"

"Because it's not fleshed out yet."

"Uh-huh." Uncertain she believed him, she bounced her tray off her thigh, and tried to see if she could find further explanation hidden in his expression. "In other words, trust you."

"Yes." He paused. "You can do that, can't you?"

Roxy didn't answer. "You want another Scotch?" she asked instead.

"Should I take that as a no?"

"Should I take that as you don't want another drink?" she countered.

"Diet cola. And when the idea is fully formed, you'll know. You don't share your order pad before bringing the drinks do you?"

The two analogies had absolutely nothing to do with one another as far as she could see. "I would if the customer asked. If they didn't like being kept in the dark."

"Fine," he said, giving an exasperated sigh. "Here." He angled his pad so she could read better. All she saw were a bunch of half sentences and notations she didn't understand.

"Satisfied?" he asked when she turned the notepad around.

Yes. Along with embarrassed. "You have terrible handwriting."

"I wasn't planning on my notes being studied. Are you always this mistrustful?"

"Can you blame me?" she replied. "I just found out my mother lied to me for thirty years."

"Twenty-nine," he corrected, earning a smirk.

"Twenty-nine. Plus, I work here. This place hardly inspires trust."

"What do you mean?"

He wanted examples? "See that table over there?" She pointed to table two where a quartet of tipsy businessmen were laughing and nuzzling with an equally tipsy pair of women. "Half those guys wear wedding bands. So does one of the women.

"You see it all the time," she continued. "Men telling women how beautiful and special they are while the entire time keeping their left hands stuffed in a pocket so no one sees the tan line." Or promising comfort when all they really wanted was a roll in the sack.

"Interesting point," Mike replied. "One difference, though. I'm not one of your bar customers."

No, she thought, looking him over. He wasn't. "I don't know you much better," she pointed out.

"You will."

Something about the way he said those two words made her stomach flutter, and made the already close atmosphere even closer. All evening long, she'd been battling a stirring awareness, and now it threatened to blossom. She didn't like the feeling one bit.

Jackie's innuendos popped into her head.

"How do you expect me to pay out?" she blurted. He frowned, clearly confused, but to her the change in topic made perfect sense. "We never talked, and last time I checked you guys don't work for free. How exactly do you expect to collect payment?"

Realization crested across his face, followed quickly by his mouth drawing into a tight line. "It's called a contingency fee," he said tersely.

"Like those personal injury lawyers that advertise on television? The ones that say you don't have to pay them until you win?"

"Exactly. What else did you expect?"

He already knew, and she felt her skin begin to color. What could she say? She was paranoid.

Life made her that way. "I didn't. Why else would I ask?"

"If you don't like that plan, you can pay hourly." He looked around the bar. "If doing so fits your budget."

Doubtful, and he knew that, too. "Your plan is fine."

"Good. Glad you approve."

"Do you still want your diet soda?"

"Please."

Shoot. She'd been hoping he'd say no, so she wouldn't have to visit his table again. "Coming right up. I'll drop it off before I cash out."

"You're done for the evening?" He straightened in his seat at the news.

Roxy nodded. The ability to clock out earlier than other bars was one of the reasons she continued working at the place. She could get home at a decent hour and be awake enough to get up with Steffi.

Reaching for his wallet, Mike pulled out a trio of bills. "This should cover my tab and tip. I'll meet you out front."

"For what?"

"To drive you home of course."

Drive her home. Maybe Jackie's comment wasn't so far off. She fingered the bills, noting his tip was beyond generous for one drink. "What's the catch?"

"No catch."

"Really?" She may have made her share of bad calls, but she wasn't stupid. Uptown lawyers didn't hang out at the Elderion and offer waitresses rides for no reason. She hadn't forgotten what he implied about her mother. "You drive all your clients home in the middle of the night?"

"If they're dressed like that, I do."

What was wrong with the way she was dressed?

"For one thing, you're not," he replied when she asked.

A comment like that was supposed to make her want to get into a car with him? "I'll have you know I've been riding the same bus for years without a single incident."

"Well, aren't you lucky."

"Luck has nothing to do with it. After a while you develop a kind of invisible armor and no one bothers you."

He frowned. "Invisible armor?"

"Street smarts, you know? People see you and realize straight off they can't hassle you. You blend in." It was outsiders like him that had to worry. Unfortunately, from the way he was already packing his things, Roxy had the distinct feeling he wasn't interested in her argument or in taking no for an answer.

What the heck. Wouldn't kill her to ride in a warm car for a change.

"I'll meet you in five," she told him.

Did she really think she was safe riding the bus wearing that outfit? Watching her sashay off, Mike rolled his eyes. For crying out loud, she wasn't even his type.

In this lifetime anyway. A memory danced on the edge of his mind. Of other late-night bus rides and willing partners. He shook it away.

"You make this commute every night?" he asked when they finally met up. She'd slipped a leather jacket over her uniform. The waist-length jacket covered her bare shoulders, but still left the legs exposed.

"Five nights a week."

They rounded the corner and headed to the pay lot, walking past the bus stop in time to see a drunken patron relieving himself on the wall. Did her invisible armor protect her from that, too? he wondered as the splash narrowly missed his shoe.

"I thought about adding a sixth," Roxy was saying, "but that would mean less time with Steffi. I hardly see her much as it is. She sees more of her babysitter."

"When you win this case, you'll have all the time in the world."

"At this point in my life I'd settle for not having to schlep drinks for a living. I don't care what they say, the smell of stale beer doesn't go away."

"You never thought of doing something else?"

"Oh, sure. I was going to be a doctor but the Elderion was too awesome to give up.

"Sorry," she quickly added. "Couldn't help myself. I could have found a day job, but originally I wanted my days free for auditions."

"Auditions? You're an actress?" A strange emotion stirred inside him. He should be concerned her career aspirations made her more interested in grabbing fifteen minutes of fame than in seeing the case through. Instead the tug felt more like envy. He chalked it up to being in the bar. The night had him thinking of old times and old aspirations.

The driver had brought out his sedan from the back of the lot. As Roxy slid into the passenger seat, her skirt bunched higher, almost to the juncture of her thighs. Mike averted his eyes while she adjusted herself. Yeah, she blended in.

"I'm impressed," he said when he settled into his driver's seat.

"Don't be. It was eight years of nothing."

"Couldn't have been that bad."

"Try worse. Turns out you need one of two things to make it in show business. Talent or cleavage. I was saving up for the latter when I had Steffi."

"So you quit for motherhood."

"Couldn't very well work all night, run around to auditions all day and take care of her, too. Since the whole acting thing wasn't working out anyway, I figured I'd cut my losses and do one thing halfway decently."

"Halfway?"

Her shrug failed to hide her embarrassment. Clearly she hadn't expected him to pick up on the modifier. "The whole 'wish I could spend more time with her' thing. Not that I have a choice, right?"

"No." He stared at the brake lights ahead of him. The city that never sleeps. Even after midnight, gridlock could snag you. "But then a lot of choices aren't really in our control."

"What do you mean?"

This time he was the one who shrugged as a way of covering up. He didn't know what he meant. The words sort of bubbled up on their own. "That a lot of the time life makes the decisions for us."

"You mean like how getting knocked up put my acting career out of its misery?" Her nonchalant expression was poorly crafted. No wonder she failed as an actress.

"She's why I'm doing all this now," she continued after a beat. "Partly anyway. I want her to have more choices than I can give her now."

This time she wasn't acting. The desperate determination in her voice was very real.

A thought suddenly occurred to him. "What about her father?"

"What about him?"

He'd hit a sore spot. He could feel her stiffen. "Is he still in the picture?"

"No."

Interesting. "Any chance he'll pop back in?"

"No."

"You sure?" Wouldn't be the first time an ex reappeared at the scent of a payday. From his point of view, the fewer complications the better.

"He's not in our lives," she repeated, her voice a little terse.

Her clenched jaw said there was more to the story. "Because he's not...?" He left the end of his sentence hoping she'd fill in the blank.

"Because he's not," she repeated. "Why are you asking anyway? I thought this case was about *my* paternity."

"It's my job to know as many details as possible about my clients."

"Even things that aren't your business?

"Everything about you is my business."

"I don't think so," she scoffed.

This was the second time tonight she'd tried to dictate what he could and couldn't discuss. Time he explained how this relationship would work. Yanking the steering wheel, he cut off the car in the next lane and pulled to the curb. "Let's get a few things straight right now. You came to me asking for help. I can't do that without your co-operation. Your. Full. Cooperation. That means if I need to know what you had for dinner last Saturday night, you need to tell me. Do you understand? Because if you can't, then this—" he waved his hand in the space between them "—isn't going to work.

"Are we clear?" he asked, looking her in the eye. Although the lecture was necessary, she could very well tell him to go to blazes. He held his breath, hoping he hadn't pushed her—and his luck—too far.

From her seat, she glared, her eyes bright in the flash of passing headlights. "Crystal."

"Good. Now I suggest you learn to deal with tough questions, because we've only scratched the surface." They were definitely revisiting her daughter's paternity, too. There was way too much emotion behind her reaction.

They drove the rest of the distance in silence, eventually pulling up in front of a nondescript building, on a street lined with them. Tall towers with squares of light, the kind of buildings his architect brother would call void of personality. At this hour of night, with the green landscaping unlit, Mike thought they had an eerie futuristic quality.

He stole a look at his companion. She hadn't moved since his lecture, her face locked on the view outside the windshield. With the shadows hiding her makeup and her hair tumbling down her back, he was surprised how classical her profile looked. Reminding him of one of those Greek busts in a museum, strong and delicate at the same time. If, that is, the pieces in the museum were gritting their teeth.

Her fingers were already wrapped around the door handle. "Want to wait till I come to a full stop or will slowing down to a crawl be good enough?" he asked her.

"Either will be fine." Her voice was tight to match her jaw. Still upset over his lecture. He added the discussion to his mental revisit list. Thing was getting pretty long. "I'll stop at the front walkway if you don't mind. Road burn never looks good on a client."

Without so much as cracking a smile, she

pointed to the crosswalk a few feet ahead. "Here is fine. I'll walk the rest of the way." She pushed open the door the moment the wheels stopped spinning. Eager to get away.

"Roxanne!" Call it guilt or anxiety over his harshness earlier, but he needed to call her back and make sure they were truly on the same page. "Do we understand each other?"

"We do." From her resignation, however, she wasn't happy about it. Never mind, she'd be happy enough with him when they settled her case.

"You still want to proceed then?" he double-checked.

She nodded, again with resignation. "I do."

"I have an opening at nine-thirty tomorrow. I'll see you then."

Resignation quickly switched to surprise. "You want to meet tomorrow?"

"Unless you'd rather meet tonight. We have a lot to go over, and you're my only source of information. Sooner we get started, the better."

Seeing her widening eyes, he added, "Is that a problem?"

"No," she replied. "No problem."

There was, but to her credit, she seemed resolved to solving whatever it was. "I'll see you at nine-thirty."

"Sharp," he added. As if he had anything better

to do. "Oh, and Roxanne? You might as well get used to spending time with me. In fact, you could say I'm about to become your new best friend."

"Great." Thrilled, she was not; he could tell by the smirk.

Surprisingly, however, he found the annoyance almost amusing. There was mettle underneath her attitude that would come in handy. Smiling, he watched her walk away, waiting till she disappeared behind the frosted front door before shifting his car into Drive. For the first time in weeks, he looked forward to a new workday. Roxanne O'Brien didn't know it yet, but she'd just become his newest and biggest priority.

He had a feeling both their futures would be better for it.

CHAPTER THREE

Roxy could feel Mike all the way to her front door and this time the sensation had nothing to do with his "presence." He was watching her.

Her new best friend. The idea was beyond laughable. She wasn't entirely sure she even liked the guy with his bossy, arrogant, elegant attitude. Add nosy, too. What business was it of his whether Steffi's father was around or not? *Everything about you is my business*. Recalling the authority in his voice, she got a hot flash. Men who could truly take charge were few and far between in her world. Most of them simply took off.

Bringing her back to Steffi's father. What a nice big bitter circle. She really did have to stop overreacting when people mentioned him. Not every remark was a reference to her bad judgment.

No, those would come later, when the Sinclairs got involved. Maybe chasing down the truth wasn't such a good idea.

Then she thought about Steffi, and her resolve returned.

Mrs. Ortega's apartment was on the third floor. The older woman met her at the door. "She give you any problems?" Roxy asked.

"Nada. Went down during her movie, same as always. She had a busy day. I had all three grandchildren."

"Sounds like a houseful."

Steffi was curled up sound asleep on the sofa, the late-night news acting as a night-light. In her hand she clutched a purple-haired plastic pony. Roxy smiled. Her daughter was in the middle of a pony fascination, the purple-haired animal not having left her hand in a month.

Carefully she scooped her up. The little girl immediately stirred. "Dusty's thirsty," she murmured, half swatting at her amber curls. Roxy wasn't quite sure she was awake.

"We'll get him some water upstairs."

"Okay." The little girl nodded and tucked her head into the crook of Roxy's neck. Her skin smelled of sleep and baby shampoo. Roxy inhaled a noseful and the scent tugged at her heart. Her little angel. Steffi might have started as a mistake, but she was the one decent accomplishment in Roxy's life. She'd do anything not to screw it up.

After making arrangements with Mrs. Ortega

for the next morning, she carried Steffi to the elevator. Stepping off onto the eleventh floor, she could hear the screech of a high speed chase playing on a television. Would it be too much to ask for it not to be her apartment?

Yes. Fumbling to balance her keys and her daughter, she opened the door to find the volume blasting. A thin, acne-prone stain wearing an orange-and-blue throwback jersey lay sprawled on the sofa. Roxy cringed. Wayne. When she first decided to take on a roommate, she figured an extra person would allow her to afford a better apartment and Alexis had been one of the few decent applicants who didn't mind living with a four-year-old. Roxy didn't realize till they signed the lease that the woman's loser brother came along with the package. He showed up at all times of the night, offering some lame excuse as to why he needed to sponge off them for the night. If she didn't need Alexis's share of the rent money, she'd kick them both to the curb.

Another reason to hope Mike Templeton was as good as he said. "Can you turn the TV down?" she whispered harshly.

"Why? The kid's asleep."

She shot him a glare. Not for long. "Because you can hear it at the elevator."

"Turn it down, Wayne." Carrying a laundry basket on her hip, his sister, Alexis, came down the hallway. "No one wants to hear that noise."

With a roll of his eyes, Wayne reached for his remote.

Alexis greeted her with a nod and dropped the basket on the dining room table. "Some guy came by looking for you. He find you?"

"Dude wouldn't stop buzzing," Wayne said. "Woke me up."

Poor baby. "Yeah, he found me," she told Alexis.

"New boyfriend?"

"No. Business. He's a lawyer who's going to be helping me with some stuff of my mother's." She flashed back to five minutes earlier, in the close confines of his car. *Better get used to my company. You and I are going to be spending a lot of time together.* Against her will, a low shiver worked its way to the base of her spine. Immediately she kicked herself. You know, Roxy, your outbursts of moral outrage might carry a little more weight if you didn't find the man attractive.

"What kind of business?" Wayne asked. "You getting money?"

"I thought you said your mother didn't leave you anything?" Alexis said. She paused. "Is this about that stuff your mother said?"

"What stuff?" Wayne asked.

Roxy ignored him. In a moment of extreme

loneliness and needing someone to talk to, Roxy had shared her mother's last words to her roommate. In fact, it was Alexis who first suggested she might have money coming to her.

"Yeah."

"He going to help you?" Her roommate's eyes became big brown saucers. Roxy swore the pupils were dollar signs. It made her reluctant to answer.

"Maybe."

She could have answered no and it wouldn't matter. Alexis had already boarded the money train and was running at high speed. "Get out. We're talking Kardashian kind of money, right? I read those Sinclairs are loaded."

"We aren't talking any kind of money." She especially wasn't talking money with the two of them. "He said he'd look into things. That's all. I have to put Steffi down before she wakes up."

It was a wonder the little girl hadn't woken up already with all the noise going on. She really must have had a busy day. Knowing her daughter had fun should have been a relief. Instead she felt a stab of guilt. She should have been the one providing the fun, not the elderly grandmother downstairs. The one who read her stories and fed her dinner. So many things she should be doing. What happened if she couldn't? Would she fade into the background like her mother, there but not there, a virtual stranger in a work uniform?

She lay her daughter in the plastic princess bed and pulled the blankets over her. Almost immediately Steffi burrowed into the mattress, Dusty the horse still gripped in her fist. Roxy brushed a curl from her cheek, and marveled at the innocence. Mike Templeton better realize how much she had riding on his ability to climb legal mountains.

"Tell me everything you can about your mother."

It was the next morning, and Roxy was sitting with her new best friend for their nine-thirty meeting. She half expected another lecture about her overreaction the night before, but he behaved as if it never happened. He even provided breakfast. Muffins and coffee, arranged neatly on his office conference table. Like they were having an indoor picnic.

"Standard client procedure?" she'd asked.

The question earned her an odd, almost evasive look that triggered her curiosity meter. "Figured you could use breakfast," he'd replied when she remarked on it.

Now he sat, legal pad at the ready, asking her about her mother. "There's not much to tell." Her mother had always been an enigma. Thanks to those letters, she was now a total stranger. "She wasn't what you'd call an open book, in case you couldn't guess." More like a locked diary.

"Let's start at the beginning. When did your parents get married?"

"June 18. They eloped."

She watched as he wrote down the date. It was barely legible. How could a man who moved his pen so fluidly have such horrendous penmanship?

"Seven months before you were born."

"Yup. To the day. I always figured I was the reason they got married."

"And you were their only child."

"One and only. I used to wish I had brothers and sisters, though. Being the only one could be lonely sometimes. Now that I think about it, that's probably one of the reasons I became an actress. I did a lot of pretending."

"Trust me, siblings aren't always great to have around," he replied.

"You have brothers and sisters?"

"One of each. And before you ask, I'm the old-est."

She wasn't sure why, but the idea he had a family intrigued her. Were they all as smooth and re-fined as he was? She pictured a trio of perfection all in navy blue blazers. "Are they lawyers, too?"

"No, I'm the only one."

"Tough act to follow, huh?"

Voice flat, he replied, "So I'm told." Another unreadable expression crossed his face. Sounded like she'd touched a nerve. Sibling rivalry or something else?

She wanted to ask more, but he steered the conversation back to being one-sided. "Your father—the one you grew up with—is he still alive?"

"Looked alive at the funeral."

Like she figured he would, he stopped writing and looked up, just in time to witness the shame creeping into her cheeks. "He took off for Florida when I was little. Guess he figured once he made a legal woman out of my mother, his job was done."

"They're divorced then."

"Good Lord, no. They were Irish Catholic. They stayed married." Instead they lived separate lives in separate states. Chained to one another by a mistake. Her.

Wonder what he'd think when he learned that he might not have had to marry her mother at all.

Mike scribbled on his notepad. "Interesting."

"What is?"

"That neither sought an annulment. If your father knew about Wentworth, he'd certainly have grounds."

"Oh." She popped a piece of muffin into her mouth, swallowing it along with the familiar defensiveness that had risen with the conversation.

Her mother's story always cut so close to home. Reminded her too much of choices she did or didn't make. She always wondered which path would have been better. Hers or her mother's?

"Maybe he didn't care," she said, as much to herself as aloud. "I always figured he wanted out as easily as possible. My mother was— I'm not sure what word I'd use."

"Quiet?"

Too simple. "Absent."

"Because she was working?"

"No. I mean, yes, she worked, but absent in a different way." She thought of all the nights she spent alone with her babysitter, nights followed by mornings where her mother would sit wordlessly with coffee and cigarettes while Roxy ate her cereal. "She was there, but not there. Like that guy in the musical, *Chicago*. Mr. Cellophane. Invisible. Only instead of being Roxy's husband, she was Roxy's mother."

She laughed at her own joke before sobering. "I always felt like part of her was missing. Guess there was."

She broke off a piece of muffin, ate it, broke off another. "She must have really loved him."

"Who?"

"Wentworth, obviously." What else would explain the change from the woman described in those letters to the ineffectual, worn-down woman Roxy grew up with? "I have no idea how much she loved my father."

"Enough to marry him."

Roxy gave him a long look. He wasn't serious, was he? "We both know there were a lot of reasons to get married that had nothing to do with being in love. First and foremost the fact she was pregnant."

With another man's child. "Think that's why he left?"

"There's only one person who knows that answer."

"I know."

Looking down, Roxy saw that while talking, she'd broken the rest of her muffin into small pieces. If ever there was a conversation worth avoiding, this was the one. Hey, Dad, I was wondering, did Mom ever mention whether you biologically deserved the title? She wasn't sure which response would be better. Him knowing, meaning yet another person kept the truth from her, or him not knowing. Which meant he really had taken off because he didn't care.

Appetite gone, she rose from the table and walked toward the window. The conference room looked across to the building next door. In one window, she could see the back of a woman as she spoke on the phone. A large potted plant sat in another. If she leaned closer to the glass and looked left, she could just see the street below.

Behind her, she heard the crinkle of leather, and a moment later the air grew warm and thick. Mike stood behind her.

Odd. At work she spent her time weaving in and out of a crowd, bodies often pressing against her. The human swarm didn't feel half as overpowering as the body heat coming from her lawyer. It was like she could feel him breathing.

He didn't say a word. He merely stood there offering silent camaraderie. Feeling him—his presence—Roxy suddenly became acutely aware they were alone and behind closed doors. Why that mattered, she wasn't sure, but it did. Maybe it was the strange urge she had to lean back and let him hold her.

"Are you close to your family?" she asked him.

"I don't see why that's relevant."

Despite not seeing his face, she could easily imagine his raised brow.

"I'm curious," she told him. And talking about her family was depressing. "Besides, I thought we were going to be each other's new best friend. Isn't that what you said last night?"

"An expression. I didn't mean we were going

to start getting our nails done and telling each other secrets."

"You have secrets?"

"No." But his answer came out stiff. She'd poked the nerve again.

Turning around, she found him standing far closer than she'd expected. No wonder she'd felt his body heat so keenly. "You don't sound very convincing."

"This meeting is about you. Not me." Again, the words and expression didn't go hand in hand. In this case, the shameful look in his copper eyes belied the stern dictate. Instead of the desired effect, it only made her more curious.

"Do they live in New York?"

"Who?"

"Your parents. Do they live in the city?"

He let out a frustrated breath, catching on that she would keep pressing until he answered. "Part of the year. They're very busy with their careers."

"They're successful like you then."

"Success is taken for granted in my family."

"Kind of like how screwing up is in mine."

"At least you have the choice."

He looked…distressed; she couldn't come up with a better word. She only knew the look didn't suit him.

He was frowning again. Never one to pay much

attention to men's mouths, she hadn't noticed before, but he had a great-looking one. Lips not too full, not too thin, with a sharply defined Cupid's bow. They weren't suited for frowning.

She raised her eyes to study the rest of his face and connected with his gaze. In that second, a spark ignited. A feeling she couldn't define but felt all the way to her toes. She found herself mesmerized by the cloudiness in his eyes, the way the brown darkened the copper-colored flecks, making them almost invisible. "You didn't have a choice?"

Her question flipped a switch, and the moment ended. The flecks returned, and he was back once again to lawyer mode. "Don't know. I make a practice of succeeding."

Roxy got the hint. Sharing time had ended. "Let's hope you don't break the streak with my case."

"I don't intend to."

He spoke with savage determination. And yet, in the back of her mind, Roxy found herself wondering exactly who the determination was meant to convince. Her?

Or himself?

CHAPTER FOUR

Dear Fiona,
I can't believe it's only been two days. Feels
like two years. You must think I'm crazy writ-
ing you again, especially after we talked half
the night, but I can't stop thinking about you.
This morning in English class, while the pro-
fessor was going over the syllabus, all I could
think of was your voice. I love your accent.
I could listen to it for hours. You don't even
have to say much. The grocery list would
work... .

TAKING off his glasses, Mike rubbed his eyes. He'd
been reading since Roxanne's departure, hoping to
get a feel of Wentworth's state of mind. He found
out. The guy had it bad. Four letters into the pile
and it was already obvious. Wonder if his parents
knew he was infatuated with one of their house-
keepers. Did they care? Was he going to find a letter later in the stack telling Fiona goodbye?

He hoped not. It would completely kill his case. Roxanne, too, since she was clearly counting on the money. Couldn't be easy waiting tables and raising a kid on your own. Taking the bus home in a skimpy uniform night after night. He didn't care how invisible she thought she was; when you showed that much leg, you weren't invisible.

Once again, a memory danced around his head. Grace Reynolds. Wow, he hadn't thought about her in years. How often did they snuggle in the last row of a bus, doing things buses weren't meant for? They almost got caught more than once. The thrill of discovery was half the fun.

Roxanne reminded him of Grace. Or rather of that time. Of course, there was a big difference between an Ivy League philosophy student and a cocktail waitress. Big difference. Must be the acting thing. The idea Roxanne chased her dream. Sure, she failed, but she still chased.

Mike couldn't remember the last time he had a dream. Least one that wasn't ordained from birth and piled heavy with expectations. Except for that one crazy semester. But that had been childish fantasy. He'd let those days go. Why were the memories coming back?

I don't know, Mike. Why did you have those thoughts this morning?

They were definitely not childish fantasies. He

didn't know what they were. One second he's talking about his family—which was none of her business—next he's looking in her eyes and thinking about how the light crowned her hair, and noting how her eyes were more a merger of earthy colors rather than simple green.

Things he had no business noticing about a client.

He'd felt this inexplicable pull the moment their eyes met.

Oh, God, listen to him. Who did he think he was, Wentworth Sinclair? His days of sparks and pulls were long gone.

Setting Wentworth's letter aside, he turned his attention to a different pile. The pile he'd been avoiding for days.

When he broke off from Ashby Gannon, everything seemed so straightforward. Templetons make things happen. They go for what they want. Wasn't that what he'd been drilled to do? Failure never entered his mind. After all, he had contacts, a proven reputation. He did all the right research. Created a business plan. Talk about arrogant overconfidence. Business plans and contacts didn't mean squat when the economy was tanking.

The first six months had been all right, but then the referrals dried up as his colleagues began keeping the work in-house. Doing "all right" became a luxury. Last month he didn't clear enough to make expenses. This month looked worse.

Which was why he needed Roxanne's case to succeed—and settle—quickly. If he could keep himself afloat until the Sinclairs made an offer, he might be all right. Otherwise...

We raised you to be better than this.

"I know, Dad," he muttered to the voice in his head. Dear Lord, did he know.

The phone rang, drowning out the thoughts. "Knew you'd be burning the midnight oil," his baby brother, Grant, said when he answered the phone. "No rest for the wicked, huh?"

Or the soon to be bankrupt. "What do you want?"

"Everything's great," Grant replied. "Thanks for asking."

"Precisely why I didn't bother asking. Everything's always going great lately." His brother was high on life at the moment.

"Can't argue with you there," Grant replied. "I'm calling to see what you're doing tomorrow night. Sophie and I thought we could all grab dinner."

Mike stilled. "Tomorrow?"

"Yeah. We thought it'd be great to talk to you in person for a change."

No, it wouldn't. Keeping up appearances was so much easier over the phone. "I can't."

He searched his brain for an excuse, the guilt hitting him before he even got the words out. "The Bar's hosting an event."

His stomach churned at the lie. This was his brother, after all. Family. He shouldn't feel the need to pretend anything with him.

Other than the fact he spent the better part of two years lecturing Grant on living up to his potential. It was getting harder and harder to pretend he had life under control in the face of his brother's newfound happiness. The reminder of his hypocrisy was too loud.

"Another one? I swear, you're a worse workaholic than my Sophie, and we know how bad she can be."

"Not everyone can afford to lounge around," he remarked, eyes falling to the stack of bills."

"I'm sure you can."

If only it were that easy. He opened his mouth to say as much, then quickly shut it. His problems were his; he'd deal with them. "I've already committed to this thing. Bought my ticket."

"Say no more. Heaven forbid you back out on an RSVP."

"Not my fault I believe in keeping my commitments." Nonexistent or otherwise.

"How about next week then?"

Again, Mike paused. The right answer was yes, of course. He had no plans. Couldn't afford them. He washed a hand over his face. "I don't know." He hated putting his brother off. "I just took on this big case and it's going to take up a lot of time...."

"Big case, hey? Anything interesting?"

Mike gave him the short version, causing the man to whistle. "Long-lost heirs. Impressive. Not your usual kind of client."

Definitely not, Mike replied in his head. "I'm branching out."

"Can't wait to hear more."

"Not much more to tell yet. I'm just drafting the initial DNA request this afternoon."

"I meant when we see you on Saturday. You can give us an update."

Closing his eyes, Mike shook his head. He wasn't going to dodge this one. "All right," he said, "I'll come by next Saturday."

"Great. I'll take care of the reservations," Grant answered. "It'll be great to catch up."

"Yeah, it will," Mike replied in a quiet voice.

They spoke a little longer, mostly about Grant's latest architectural project, which was going spectacularly. As he listened, Mike tried to remind himself Grant had floundered for two whole years, and his returning to architecture was to be celebrated. He hated the part of him that twisted with envy. He was happy for him. Truly.

After promising for a second—and third—time he would keep their next date, he hung up. No sooner did the phone line click dead than he found his thoughts right back to Roxanne. When she left this morning, she'd promised to make a phone call of her own. To Florida to ask her father about Wentworth. He didn't envy the task. *Are you close to your parents?* Her question came floating back, along with the note in her voice that made her sound so very small and vulnerable. The memory alone was enough to tug at him. He'd never had a client get to him like this before. Then again, he'd never had a client this important before, either. Grant was right: she wasn't his usual client.

She was way, way more.

"Don't look now, but your lawyer's back."

Hearing Jackie's announcement, Roxy nearly dropped her tray. "Mike's here?" Sure enough, he sat at the same table as before in the same blue blazer as this morning. Recalling how closely she'd stood to those buttons, Roxy felt a shiver go through her. "What does he want?"

"Better be a drink," Dion replied. "We aren't

here so he can set up shop and take the table away from paying customers."

Roxy ignored him. She was too busy watching Mike as he folded his coat over the back of a chair. Why on earth would he drive across town for a second night in a row?

Only one way to find out. Soon as she unloaded the drinks on her tray, she made her way to his table. Just like last night, he was scribbling away on a yellow legal pad. "Is there a problem?"

He looked up, so unsuited for a bar like this it wasn't funny. It caused her breath to catch. "Why would there be a problem?" he asked.

"Because you're here."

"Felt like a Scotch."

An incomplete answer if ever she heard one. "Don't they serve liquor in your neck of the woods?"

"They do, but I like this place. It reminds me of somewhere I used to spend time."

Really? The idea of Mike Templeton anywhere near a bar like the Elderion on a regular basis boggled her mind. She covered her surprise with a shrug. "It's a free country." Though she had to wonder.

"Wait." She paused midturn. "This isn't about my taking the bus home is it? Because I told you already—"

"You take the bus all the time. Don't worry, I got that message loud and clear."

"Good. I hate having to repeat myself."

"Wouldn't want that, would we." He was looking over the rim of his glasses at her. The way the light reflected off the lenses made reading his eyes impossible so she couldn't tell if his tone was sarcastic or not.

"Although I have to ask," he continued. "Would it be so awful if I did bring you home?"

No, her mind immediately answered. Wow, talk about old mistakes rearing their ugly head. As if she'd let anyone take her home again. "I'll go get your Scotch."

"I did come by for a reason."

Ah, she knew there was something. She waited for him to explain.

"I wanted to let you know I plan to submit the DNA request on Monday."

"So soon?" Her heart stopped. The crowd around them receded, drowned out by the wind tunnel sounding in her ears. She hadn't expected things to move so quickly. "I haven't reached my father yet." A sinking sensation erupted in her stomach. Could she still call him her father?

"You'll reach him soon enough. The Sinclairs will reject this request out of hand anyway giving you plenty of time. We're really filing so they know we exist. Once we make our position clear, we can force an offer."

"Offer?" She was confused. "I thought we were asking for a DNA test."

"We are."

He motioned for her to sit down. After glancing over to make sure Dion wasn't paying attention, Roxy complied.

"This is our opening move. They'll react. We'll counteract, and so on, till we get what we want."

"You're talking about the money."

"Exactly."

"Where does the DNA test come in?"

"It doesn't."

"But—" She was lost. "Are you saying there won't be a DNA test?"

Mike looked up from his paperwork. "Not if we accept a settlement offer first."

"Wait a second. Without a test, how will I know for certain whether Wentworth is my father?"

"Does it matter?"

Yes, it mattered. She didn't realize until this moment but it mattered a lot. "Did you think I only wanted the money?"

"Basically, yes."

In other words, his opinion from the other day hadn't changed at all. He still thought her a gold-digging fraud. Worst part of it was she'd gone to him about the money. She had no one to blame for his opinion but herself.

"I've got tables to wait on." She couldn't deal with this right now. Not at work. Blindly she headed into the crowd, colliding with the first body that crossed her path.

"Hey," a nasal-voiced brunette whined. "Watch where you're going."

"Sorry," Roxy muttered.

"Look what you did. You made me spill my drink!"

"I'll get you a new one." More charges against her paycheck.

"Damn right, you're getting me a free drink." Based on the way her words slurred, she didn't need one, either. "And a new blouse. Did you see what you did?" She gave a wobbly wave across her torso. A blue splash, about waist-high, marred the orange silk. "This is designer! Do you know how much it cost?"

Full price or discount? Roxy would bet she didn't pay retail. She knew the woman's type.

Still, the customer was always right. "Send the bill to the guy in the blue blazer," she told the woman. "He's the money man."

The brunette squinted in confusion. "What?"

"Just send us the bill." More charges for Dion to deduct from her paycheck. At this rate, she might as well be working for free. Trying to move on, she attempted to sidestep the woman, but unfortunately, the brunette wasn't ready to let the topic drop. "I want to talk to a manager," she slurred. Came out more like *I wannatalkamanger*. "Someone's going to pay for my blouse."

"Like I said, send us the dry-cleaning bill, and we'll gladly take care of it."

"Dry cleaners? What's a dry cleaner going to do? This shirt's ruined."

Pul-leeze. The stain wasn't that big. Dion would tell the woman the same exact answer. She turned around, planning to head to the bar and get him. The brunette, thinking she was walking away, grabbed her arm. "Don't you walk away from me."

She attempted to yank Roxy around. Stopping short on her heels, Roxy instead stumbled backward, bumping shoulders with the woman and causing more cocktail to splash.

"You stupid idiot!" the woman shrieked. Blue liquid stained her bare arm. "Look at what you did now! How would you like it if I spilled a drink all over you?"

There was maybe a half an inch left in her martini glass. Rearing back, the woman tossed the liquid at Roxy's face. An arm appeared out of nowhere and grabbed Roxy's waist, pulling her safely out of the line of fire.

She didn't need to look to see who the arm belonged to. The way her insides reacted was identification enough.

"Come on, Roxy," Mike murmured in her ear, "let's go get you some air."

"Why are you pulling me away?" she protested as he dragged her toward the front door. "I didn't start the fight."

"No, but I didn't want to take the chance of you sticking around and letting the situation escalate. Last thing we need is an article in the *Daily Post* about you getting into a bar fight."

"News flash, I work in a bar." She yanked her arm free. What did a news article matter anyway?

Oh, right. The lawsuit. He didn't want bad publicity impacting his "settlement."

A blast of cold air hit her, a harsh reminder spring was still a few weeks away. "Here." Before she could say a word, she found herself enveloped in a blue worsted-wool cocoon. Despite her annoyance, she wrapped the blazer around her with gratitude.

"She started it," she muttered.

"Technically you started it when you stormed into the crowd. You've got to stop overreacting to everything I say. Or—" he adjusted the jacket on her shoulders "—at least stop storming off before we're done talking. Do you want to explain what I said this time that was so wrong?"

"Isn't it obvious?"

"Honestly, not really. The other night you talked about wanting to make a better life for your daughter. I assumed you meant financially."

"I did." After all, it was the Sinclair money that would help her help Steffi, not the bloodline. Truth be told, she didn't understand her reaction completely herself except that as soon as he talked about not going through with the DNA test, her blood ran cold. She didn't realize until that moment how badly she wanted—she needed—to know the truth. Needed to know how and why she was brought into this world. If she was created out of love or simply created.

She hugged the jacket tighter. The cloth smelled of bar soap and musk-scented aftershave, exactly how she expected his clothes to smell.

Meanwhile, Mike had moved over to the curb where he stood studying the traffic. Realizing she was seeing him in shirtsleeves for the first time, she took a good look. Without the extra layer he looked different. More exposed, more human. The broadcloth pulled taut across his shoulders and back, revealing a body that was lean and muscular. Bet if she touched him, it would feel like chiseled rock. She doubted a man like him, with so many assets, could understand her desire. "I can't explain why, but knowing makes a difference."

"You know that makes the case a whole lot more difficult," he said.

"I know."

Joining him, she touched his shoulder. "Not knowing for certain would haunt me. I want to be able to tell Steffi where she came from." She wanted to know herself.

"You're the client." He washed a hand across his features. "If you want a DNA test, then we push for a DNA test."

Roxy smiled. She knew his acquiescence had everything to do with her wishes as his client and not for her personally, but at the moment she didn't care. It just felt good to have her wishes heard.

The bar door opened, and Jackie's ponytailed head peered around the corner. "Hey, Rox, you comin' back in or what? We're swamped here."

"I'll be right there," Roxy replied. To Mike, she said, "Your idea of disaster is bad publicity, but mine is getting fired. Bills still need to be paid."

He half nodded in response. "I know what you mean."

Doubtful, but she appreciated the attempt at commiseration. There was another gust of wind and musk teased her nostrils, reminded her that the warmth around her shoulders belonged to him. Reluctantly she moved to shed his jacket.

"Keep it on till you get inside," Mike told her.

"You sure? A drink might come flying in my direction when I walk through the door."

"I'll take my chances," he replied, flashing a smile.

"Thank—" Her answer drifted off as she found herself caught in his coppery eyes. The gentle reassurance swirling in the brown depths caught her breath. All of a sudden her lungs felt too big for her chest, as if some giant balloon had expanded. The air hummed with energy and the sound of their breathing. What happened to the traffic? Surely the world hadn't disappeared leaving only the two of them.

Or had it? The spark, that inexplicable connecting spark from this morning resurrected itself. Her gaze dropped to his mouth. She heard a hitch and realized, without having to look, that his gaze had dropped, too. He was studying her mouth. Did he like what he saw? She did. Her body swayed a little bit closer. Close enough to put them both in a very dangerous position.

CHAPTER FIVE

WHAT are you doing, Templeton? Mike didn't know. In front of him, Roxanne's lips glistened invitingly. He couldn't tear his eyes away. The strong connection he felt this morning had returned, and he was trapped in its pull. Thoughts raced through his head. Wild, crazy thoughts like pressing her against the brick wall and kissing her until their lungs ran out of air. And more.

He didn't have these kinds of thoughts. Not anymore. He certainly shouldn't be having them now.

"This is a mistake." He delivered his verdict in a whisper, part of him wondering if he was speaking quietly on purpose. To avoid hearing his own warning. Roxanne heard, though, and relief filled her face. Clearly she agreed.

Whether the tightness in his gut was relief or disappointment, he refused to say.

He was pretty sure he knew the answer when she looked away and the tightness grew. "I better get inside before Dion has my head," she said in a soft voice. She shrugged off his jacket and handed it to him. "You should take this back," she said. "I can't afford the dry-cleaning bill."

"Yet," he corrected, hoping the teasing would bring back some of the connection.

"Yet," she repeated.

That was another thing. Agreeing to push for the DNA test. All he did was postpone any settlement offers, delaying payment. He couldn't afford to delay. Like the lady said, you still got to pay the bills.

But listening to her, the way she was trying so hard to keep her voice from quivering, he knew he had to say yes. He wanted her to have her answers.

Why was he suddenly feeling so invested in her results? What happened to the invisible wall between lawyer and client? To focusing on using this case to regain his financial footing? Was nostalgia getting to him?

Or a set of soft red curls, he asked himself, fingers twitching to touch them.

He pulled himself back to business. "Hopefully no one took my paperwork while we were outside talking," he said. "I can see your boss tossing them out so someone else could sit down."

"Me, too," Roxanne replied, rewarding him with a smile. Mike felt a wave of something rolling over him, settling dangerously near his chest. Whatever had him acting out of character—nostalgia or the curls—it was getting stronger.

Maybe instead of worrying about paperwork, he should worry about that instead.

Roxy clicked off her cell phone and let it drop to her lap. Just her luck. Her father had taken off for a fishing trip in the Bahamas, and no one was sure when he would return. So much for getting answers from him. He wasn't even available by cell; she had to leave a message with his lady "friend".

And she'd been worried about blindsiding him so soon after her mother's death. She should have realized. After all, this was the man who, when she told him about being pregnant said, "What do you want me to do?"

Her fingers played with the edge of her phone case. She'd told Mike she'd give him an update after she called. Updating, however, meant talking to each other, which she'd been avoiding doing the past three days. She'd even gone so far as to ignore his phone calls.

"A mistake." His words floated back. Actually they never left. She'd been hearing them loud and clear since he whispered them Friday night. A mistake. Story of her life.

He was right, of course. They had been teetering on the brink of a very bad idea. She had absolutely no business kissing the man, no matter how compassionate he seemed or how drawn she was to him. Seeking reassurance in a man's arms was a dangerous idea with ramifications that lasted a lifetime. She should know. Assuming, of course, things had gone further than a kiss. What made her think he was remotely interested? Why would he be?

Desire and loneliness. The worst combination in the world. Made a person make stupid decisions. Like reaching out for the wrong person or seeking solace in the wrong places. Problem was desire only killed loneliness for a short time. Then the sun came up leaving you to deal with the fallout. She'd learned that lesson the hard way four years ago.

Clearly Mike's resolution saved them both a lot of potential problems. Now if she could only shake the needy, lonely ache in her chest.

A purple-and-white blur danced before her face. Blinking back to earth, she smiled at her little girl, who was making her pony dance through the air.

"Can I have a cookie?" Steffi asked.

"After dinner," Roxy replied. The answer earned her a pout. "If you're really hungry, you can have orange chips." Orange chips were her way of selling sliced carrots as a snack. Sometimes the trick worked; sometimes it didn't.

Today looked to be a hard sell. "Wayne bought potato chips."

"I don't think Wayne would want us touching his things without asking," she replied. Talk about irony. Wayne sure didn't have a problem with touching others' stuff. "We have orange chips. Would you like some?"

"Okay." Enthusiastic, the response was not. "Can Dusty have some, too?"

"Sure." If it would help her daughter eat better. "We'll give him his own bowl so he can share with the other ponies. And," she added, "if you're both good and eat them all up, we can have macaroni and cheese for supper."

"Yay!" Satisfied she'd won something—in her little mind, mac and cheese was boxed gold— her daughter went back to her farm set. A half dozen ponies lay on their sides on the floor in front of the red plastic barn. "The horses are having a sleepover," she explained in an important voice.

"I better get the chips then. They might get hungry."

"Chips, chips, chips," Steffi chanted, pretending the cheer came from the horses.

While she watched her daughter chatter and play, a lump worked its way into Roxy's throat. Today was the way every day should be. Filled with mommy-daughter time and pretend pony games. If it were up to her, Steffi would never go a day unhappy. Or feeling unwanted. She'd wake up every day knowing the world was glad she existed.

If she had one regret in this world it was that Steffi didn't have a father who knew what a joy the little girl was. At the moment her daughter was too young to wonder too much about her dad. Eventually, though, she would, and Roxy would be forced to tell her the truth. Then what?

Hopefully she could at least give her a grandfather.

In her chest, the lonely feeling grew. She squeezed her phone. Go on, call him. You know you want to.

That was the problem. In spite of her avoidance, she wanted to talk with him. Worse, she wanted to feel his body close to hers again, and lose herself in the coppery concern of his eyes. She wanted to carry through on that kiss. So much for hard lessons learned, eh?

The front door buzzed while she was putting the bag of sliced carrots back in the fridge.

"Roxanne?" called the voice on the other end.

Her insides took a pathetic little tumble. She cursed herself. "Mike?" she repeated, as if she really needed to identify him. "What are you doing here?"

"Hoping to talk with you obviously. I've been trying to reach you all day."

"My phone's been off," she lied.

There was a pause. "Oh. May I come up?"

Did she have a choice? She buzzed him in.

Soon as she did, all her mental berating went out the window. Her heart sped up at the prospect of seeing him. Quickly she scanned the apartment. The place looked terrible. Folded laundry sat in a basket in the hall waiting to be put away. Steffi's toys littered the floor—the farm took up a lot of real estate. A half-drunk juice box and bowls of carrots on the floor. Picture books on the couch. How fast could she straighten up? Or did she straighten herself up instead? Change the yoga pants and T-shirt she'd tossed on this morning. And makeup! She wasn't wearing a stitch! She was a bigger mess than the apartment. Get a grip, Roxy. Bad idea, remember?

He knocked. She jumped.

"Mommy, someone's at the door," Steffi announced, not moving from the floor.

"I know, baby." Stupid elevator would be fast for once. Combing her fingers through her hair, she prayed whatever brought him here was important enough to make him oblivious to his surroundings.

Opening the door, she realized instantly it wouldn't matter if he was oblivious or not. No amount of sprucing would make her or the apartment worthy. He'd still outclass the place.

"What's up?" she asked, forcing a casual note into her voice. She could at least act unaffected, right?"

A challenge as he strode inside the same way he entered the bar. Like he owned the place. "I met with Jim Brassard today," he said.

"Who's Jim Brassard?"

"Managing partner at—" He stopped short when he saw Steffi. Her daughter was squatting in front of her farm, staring up at him with Dusty clutched protectively in her fist.

"Baby, this is Michael," Roxy said. "He's a… friend…of Mommy's."

Mike arched a brow at the word friend, but made no correction. "Hello, Steffi."

For a second, Roxy thought he might stick out his hand to go along with his formal greeting. Instead the two of them had a mini stare-off. Steffi won. Mike looked back up at her, with a silent "What now?"

"Mike and I have some business we need to talk about at the table. Can you play with your ponies while we talk?"

Wordlessly Steffi went back to her farm, but not before casting another look in Mike's direction from over her shoulder.

"She looks like you," Mike remarked, shedding his overcoat. He'd given up the winter camel hair in favor of a trench coat that hung unbuttoned over a different shade gray suit. Eyeing the peach-colored shirt, Roxy did her best not to think about the body she glimpsed the other night. Naturally she failed.

"Can I get you some coffee or something?" she asked, still acting unaffected. It felt weird watching him settle in as if this were his home. He so clearly didn't fit.

"We're not at the bar," he replied. "You don't have to serve me." He moved to sit down only to shoot back up. Reaching down, he held up a plastic duck.

Roxy's cheeks warmed. "Sorry. The chair doubles as the farm pond. Steffi, can you come get Mr. Quack Quack? I think he's done swimming."

Wordlessly Steffi trotted over and plucked the critter from Mike's fingers before settling back in front of her farmhouse. Mr. Quack Quack, Roxy noticed, found a home on her lap where he couldn't be touched.

"We don't get a lot of visitors," she whispered to Mike, feeling the need to explain. "Make's her a little shy. So long as you don't mess up her farm animals you should be fine."

"Don't worry. I think the farm is safe."

Seeing he'd settled in and had his briefcase on the table, Roxy switched to business mode. "So you talked to this Jim person," she prodded.

"Jim Brassard from Brassard, Lester. He manages the Sinclair sisters' legal affairs. I remember him from when I was at Ashby Gannon. He's sharp. Very old school, too."

Roxy wasn't sure she liked the term "old school." "What did he say?"

"About what I expected. I presented our evidence and requested a test. He said no."

Roxy's heart sank. He told her to expect a denial, but a part of her still hoped the news would be welcomed with open arms. Foolish, she knew, but wouldn't it have been nice?

The end of the table's veneer edging had come unglued, so she picked at it nervously. "What now?"

"We wait and see," he replied. "I laid some solid groundwork today. Plus, Brassard recognizing me from Ashby Gannon helped. Helped him realize he's not dealing with some ambulance-chasing creep."

"To fight uptown, you gotta go uptown," she mumbled.

"What?"

"Nothing. Something I told myself once."

"Keep in mind," he said, "we've only just

started. This was our preliminary salvo. If you want your DNA test, we need to show them we aren't going away.

"You still want to push for the test, right?" he asked.

Roxy looked to the little girl playing nearby. Playing Mike's way—for the money—would ensure her little girl's future. But she deserved to know something about where she came from. "Yes," she answered without doubt. "I want to know. Steffi needs to know her mother wasn't…" She paused, the thought too painful to say aloud. "I want to know."

Returning to playing with the veneer, she kept her eyes more focused on the chipped plastic than on the man across from her. His scrutiny felt more intense than ever. Who knew what looking into his eyes would make her feel. "I—" she heard him start.

Roxy gave in and looked up. "Yes?"

"Never mind. Back to Jim's response. His refusal means we'll need to step things up on our own end."

"How?" Her attention was aroused.

"Legally he can refuse our request until the cows come home. The law is very specific about the amount of time you have to bring a claim against an estate, and you're well past the deadline."

Story of her life. Too little. Too late. "What can we do then?"

He clicked his black lacquer pen. "Way I see things, our best approach is to mount a two-prong approach. We file the appropriate legal challenges and wait for them to wend their way through court—which could take years, by the way."

"What's the other prong?"

"We increase public pressure. Force the Sinclairs to act in the interest of good public relations."

She waited while he rummaged through his briefcase, coming up with his yellow legal pad. The pages were half-filled by this point and he had to flip several over until he reached a blank sheet. When he did, he folded his hands and leaned forward.

Roxy leaned forward, too. There was a cautiousness to his movements that made her wary. She wanted to make sure she didn't miss a word. "What exactly do you want to do?"

Those coppery eyes sparkled, completely not helping her cause. Making matters worse, he slowly raised the left corner of his mouth, creating a lopsided, sexy smile.

"We talk to the press."

Mike had hoped the fact she'd been an actress would mean Roxanne would be fairly receptive to his idea. He'd hoped wrong. Immediately her attention went to the little girl playing nearby. "Won't talking to the press tick them off?"

"There is a risk," he conceded. "But going public also lets us tell our side of the story."

"You mean mine," she corrected. "*My* side of the story. You're not going to be the one sharing your life history."

"No, I'm not." She was right about that.

He watched her chew the inside of her cheek, an action that turned her mouth into an uneven, yet still amazingly appealing, pout. Without makeup she looked a lot younger than twenty-nine. Sure, there were circles under her eyes from keeping late hours, but the fatigue was offset by a newly acquired innocence. The vulnerability he always sensed lurking had risen to the surface. She looked softer. Sweeter. Dangerous words to use when describing a client, especially when he spent the better part of the past couple of days reminding himself a good lawyer did not pursue his clients. They did not kiss them. And they especially didn't fantasize about taking late-night bus rides and reliving college age exploits.

So of course, when she didn't return his calls, he went across town for a face-to-face meeting so he could battle those thoughts all over again. As if he couldn't be more distracted.

"It's a good strategy." For the case's sake, he forced himself to stay on topic. "Going public prevents them from sweeping you or your request under the rug."

No sale. He could tell by the way her eyes went from mostly green to mottled brown.

Seriously, did he really know her mood based on eye color?

Why was she so against the idea anyhow? She'd wanted to be an actress, for crying out loud. This was her shot to be in the limelight.

There was a rattle of plastic behind him. Her daughter fixing a plastic fence, mumbling something to the plastic purple-and-white pony about not getting lost.

Of course. He bet her reaction went back to their conversation the other night regarding Steffi's father. "You know," he said, "another benefit to talking to the press is that you get to be proactive. You can control the message." He indicated Steffi with a flicker of his eyes.

Picking up on his point immediately, she crossed her arms. "You promised to leave her out of this."

Now her eyes were green. A very angry shade of green. Her whisper was equally harsh. "I told you I didn't want her involved."

"What I said was I'd do my best." He decided not to point out her wish had been completely un-realistic.

"Well, if this is your best, then you suck." Shoving her chair so hard it nearly tipped over, she marched into the kitchen. From behind the dividing wall, Mike heard the sound of pots and cupboards being slammed about.

Feeling scrutinized, he looked over to find Steffi staring at him with wide, accusing eyes. Great. The kid was mad at him, too. What was he supposed to do?

"Your mother is… Um, that is, she and I…" The girl continued to stare.

Dammit. He'd have an easier time getting through to Roxanne.

"You've got to stop the storming off," he said, joining her in the kitchen. "It makes having a conversation very difficult."

She stood at the kitchen sink filling a saucepan with water. "I promised Steffi macaroni and cheese."

"At this exact moment?"

"Better than making her wait. Not like we had anything more to talk about."

Mike rolled his eyes. "I thought you were past arguing with me about everything I want to do?"

"You thought wrong." She slapped off the faucet and lifted the pan from the sink. The motion caused her T-shirt skimming the waistband of her pants to rise, too, creating yet another invitation to look at her behind. Damn if he wasn't developing a fixation for studying the woman's body.

He fanned his fingers in his hair, tugging the roots as a way of forcing his eyes upward. "Look, I get it. You want to protect your child. But surely you realized you couldn't keep her existence a secret forever. Brassard's investigators would find her in two seconds."

"Of course I didn't think I could keep her a secret."

"Then what?" There was a small space of countertop between the stove and sink. He leaned against it, fingers curling around the Formica lip, and waited while she adjusted the burner. "Is it because you're embarrassed?"

"What? No! How can you even say that? Steffi's the best thing I ever accomplished. I could never be embarrassed of her."

Not of her, maybe. But of something else? Her angry reaction the other night came home to roost. "Is it her father then?"

Roxanne slapped the lid on the saucepan with a clank so loud he wondered if she wanted the water to boil faster or let off steam. "I told you, Steffi's father's out of the picture."

Out, but not forgotten. "Wouldn't be the first time an absentee parent crawled out of the woodwork at the scent of money."

"He wouldn't."

So she said the other night. "You can't be certain."

"Yes, I can. In order to crawl anywhere he'd have to know she exists."

"He doesn't know?"

"No." She'd crossed the room and was manically moving boxes around an upper cabinet. "I couldn't tell him."

Mike couldn't see her face, but he could hear the tension in her voice. She was literally gritting her teeth. "What do you mean you couldn't tell him?" Didn't she mean wouldn't? "Is he dead? Married?"

She laughed at his suggestions, hollow and without humor, but didn't answer. It was like pulling teeth.

"I need to know," he pushed. "If there's any chance the Sinclairs can dig up the information, then you need to tell me."

"I couldn't tell him because I don't know his last name." She choked on the answer, the words barely getting out. "I'm not a hundred percent sure of his first name, either."

It took a moment for him to process her reply. When he finally did, he was shocked at how viscerally he reacted. His chest burned with anger against the man. "You're saying—"

"I got drunk and knocked up by a total stranger? Yeah, that pretty much sums up the story." She was trying to sound indifferent, as though it was no big deal, and having no luck. Hearing the same in her voice, his anger toward this faceless stranger rose. He hurt for her. If he could take away her embarrassment and shame he would.

His hand barely closed over her shoulder when she shrugged him away. "Like mother like daughter, right?" she said bitterly.

"What happened?" Much as he didn't want to ask, he had to know. For the case, he told himself.

"What do you think happened? I'd had a really lousy day so I went to the lounge to drown my sorrows. This guy offered a shoulder and free drinks. He was gone when I woke up."

Mike balled his fist. What kind of man wouldn't want to be there when she woke up?

"Least I got Steffi out of the deal." Again, she failed at nonchalance. Mike blamed the unshed tears brimming in her eyes.

"She doesn't know obviously. When she asks about her father, I can usually distract her."

Sniffing back the emotion, she reached up with a shaky hand and closed the cabinet door. "Don't know what I'll tell her when she gets older."

Finally the pieces were coming together. "You're afraid she'll learn the truth."

"What if I embarrass her?" she asked in a voice so small it kicked him square in the gut.

Unlikely, given the girl was four years old and could be kept sheltered, but he understood the fear nonetheless. More than she realized. "No one wants to let down the people they love. To think you failed them."

"You must think you picked a real winner of a client."

He had to hold back the urge to cup her chin and force her to meet his eyes. "Actually I think I picked just fine. Way I see it, you're simply a woman who made a mistake. Hardly the first."

"The second in my family alone," she remarked. "Least my mother and Wentworth could say they were in love. I can pretend he would have been happy about the news."

Whereas her other father what? Wasn't?

That's why the DNA test was so important to her. She needed context. A better legacy to give her daughter.

Emotions that had been shoved to the background years before began to unfurl, and in that moment he found himself looking not at a client or even a physically attractive woman, but a person, alone and hurting. He understood her fear. She was afraid of letting her daughter down, because doing so might mean losing her as well.

Yeah, he understood that fear all too well. Suddenly winning her case became doubly important, becoming as much about helping her as it did about saving his own failing hide. He would do anything in his power to make sure she got everything she deserved.

Halfway across the kitchen, he stopped. The strength of his conviction frightened him. She was a client, for goodness' sake. She shouldn't be so damn important. She shouldn't be anything more than the means to an end.

Yet, here he was closing the space between them with the singular thought of taking her in his arms.

"Mommy?" There was the sound of small feet approaching the doorway. Mike immediately stiffened and moved away. Roxy did the same.

Steffi appeared in the doorway. "Dusty and I finished our chips," she announced. "Can we have our macaroni cheese now?"

"Sure, baby," Roxy replied. She still hadn't turned around. Mike saw her swiping at her cheek. "I'm making it right now. How about you go wash your hands, okay?"

"Okay." The little girl shot a look in his direction before turning around. He didn't think four-year-olds had accusing glares, but he'd been wrong. She clearly blamed him for her mother's unusual behavior.

On the stove, the saucepan cover rattled. "Don't know why I bother to tell her to wash her hands," Roxy said, giving a large sniff. "She's going to grab that horse again, and goodness knows how many germs are on that thing."

She was grasping at normalcy, pretending the earlier conversation didn't happen. Needing the reprieve himself, he let her. He returned to his spot next to the stove. "I take it she loves horses."

"What gave you your first clue?" Macaroni cascaded from the box into boiling water. "Right before the holidays I took her to Central Park and she saw the carriages. Since that moment it's been all horses all the time. I'm not sure, but I think she wants to move into that farm."

"Has she been to the stables in the park yet?"

"No. I'd like to, but I'm concerned she'll want to sign up for riding lessons and I'm not sure when I'll be able to afford them. I hate saying 'maybe... we'll see.' Feels like such a cop-out."

"My sister, Nicole, took lessons," he told her. "Did the whole jumping and riding around the circle thing."

"Was she any good? Wait, let me guess." She cast him a look from over her shoulder. "She was excellent."

"Made the junior Olympic team in high school."

"Impressive."

Not really. Not when you stopped to think there hadn't been any other choice but to excel. A hobby's not worth doing, unless done right, his parents always said.

He followed her back to the dining room table and watched as she lay down the plates in a neat triangle. "How about you? What activity did you dominate?" she asked. "Football? Debate team?"

"Swimming. I was fourth in the all-city eight-hundred meter butterfly my senior year."

He didn't tell her how disappointed his parents had been at the results or how much he hated the sport. Mike had actually wanted to take fencing. A late-night swashbuckler movie had him convinced sword fighting would be the best hobby ever. But his father had been on the swim team in college. Besides, he'd been clumsy in fencing class, enthusiastic but uncoordinated, where as the swimming instructor noted he had natural ability. Unable to fit both in his schedule, fencing class got dropped in favor of the sport with more potential.

He probably wouldn't have enjoyed fencing all that much anyway.

"We're ready, Mommy." Steffi returned. As predicted, the purple-and-white pony was clutched firmly in her hand.

"Dusty wash his hands, too?"

"Uh-huh." The little girl nodded and placed her pony next to one of the plates. Then and only then did Mike realize the table was set for three. Roxanne must have noticed, too, because she suddenly became quite interested in tucking her hair behind her ear. "I wasn't thinking. Would you like to stay for dinner?"

"He can't," Steffi piped in. "He didn't eat any orange chips."

Mimicking the stance her mother had held a few minutes earlier, the little girl crossed her arms in front of her chest.

"Mike and I are going to eat ours with dinner," Roxy replied. Then, as if realizing she'd made an assumption again, her cheeks grew pink. "That is, if you want…"

"Sure." After all his thoughts in the kitchen, he'd probably be better off going home, but he needed to finish their conversation about talking to the press. "Although…" He leaned toward her. "Orange chips?"

"Don't worry," Roxanne replied. "You'll be fine."

Considering the fact his hand still twitched to touch her, Mike wondered.

Orange chips, it turned out thankfully, were

nothing more than presliced carrots, which Roxanne thoughtfully steamed.

The meal itself was fairly quiet. Still in judgment mode, Steffi kept a close eye on whether or not he ate his carrots. Mike made a point of eating several forkfuls quickly. Wasn't much choice if he wanted to eat his meal without continual scrutiny. The gesture seemed to mollify her, and she soon focused on her own food.

Her mother on the other hand… Out of the corner of his eye, he stole a look at the woman poking at the pasta on her plate. Although the dinner invitation had been her idea, she had been strangely withdrawn since serving the food. Mike couldn't blame her. He felt a little awkward himself, the realizations from the kitchen still churning up his insides.

Across the table, Steffi dipped her pony's nose in the yellow sauce.

"Don't put your toys in your food," Roxanne told her.

"Dusty's drinking the cheese."

"Steffi."

"Okay." She dragged the word out to two syllables before turning her scrutiny back on him. "You're not eating your macaroni."

"I, um…" How did he tell the girl he didn't like

her favorite meal? Especially when he already felt dangerously close to her bad side.

Roxanne saved the day. "Stop worrying about what Mike's doing, and focus on your own meal. Do you want some more?"

Mouth slick with bright yellow cheese, Steffi nodded. "Wayne ate two boxes of macaroni cheese."

"Wayne?" Mike asked, perking up.

"My roommate's brother. He's the one who answered the buzzer when you came by the other evening. And when did you see Wayne eat macaroni and cheese?"

"This morning. When you were taking a shower."

Mike remembered Wayne now. Mr. Personality. "He's here in the morning?"

"He's here all the time," Roxanne replied, scraping half her plate's contents onto her daughter's.

"He uses bad words," Steffi piped in.

"Yes, he does, and don't talk with your mouth full. Bad words are the least of his sins," Roxanne told him. "I thought sharing costs with a roommate would be a good idea, but..." She shrugged, letting him fill in the rest of the sentence.

The woman was entirely too hard on herself, Mike decided. Although, Wayne might serve one good purpose. "That's another reason to go public. Could get you out of this arrangement that much faster."

She sat back in her chair, fork twisting between her fingers. At least she was considering the point. Meant he was making some headway.

Dinner finished. Mike was just standing to help clear the dishes when a key jingled in the lock. The door opened, and a young couple walked in, one a chunky, unnatural blonde, the other a bony punk wearing a zippered sweater and oversize plaid baseball cap. Both zeroed in on him straight away.

The infamous Wayne and his sister he presumed.

Alexis was the first to greet him, coming around to lean against his side of the table. "Hey," she said, flipping her hair over her shoulder.

Meanwhile Wayne made a beeline for the couch where he immediately threw himself down and turned on the television set. The sound of a reality TV argument filled the apartment.

"Ignore him," the roommate—Alexis he remembered her name being—said. "He's ticked off because he lost money."

From the couch Wayne issued an obscene-laden complaint against spring baseball, proving Roxanne's comment about bad language.

"Told you not to bet on them, idiot," Alexis shot back. She smiled and leaned backward a little more. The change in position caused her back to arch, and her breasts, both ample and on display, to thrust upward. "You must be Roxy's lawyer. The one who's going to make her rich."

From the corner of his eye he saw Roxanne wince, and his sympathy went out to her. "You mean, am I trying to help her prove Wentworth Sinclair is her father? Yes, I am."

"And how is that going?" the blonde asked.

"I'm afraid I can't talk about cases with anyone but my clients."

"Not even with your client's roommate?"

"Not even with her."

"How—" she flipped her hair again "—considerate of you."

"It's the law, idiot," Wayne said. "He can't talk about his cases. Don't you watch television?"

"Doesn't mean he can't be considerate, too," Alexis shot back. She smiled. "Right?"

Mike glanced around the table. Still in her chair, Steffi had gone back to watching him, as if waiting for his response. Meanwhile, Roxanne was nowhere to be seen. A noise in the kitchen told him that's where she escaped. Quickly he snatched up his plate and Steffi's now empty one. "Roxanne is waiting for these," he said following suit.

"So that's the infamous Wayne and his sister, hey?"

She stood at the sink, again filling the saucepan, this time with soapy water. "I hate that Sophie is growing up around people like him," she muttered. Him, meaning Wayne. "I can't wait until I can afford to get out of here."

"You know how you can speed up the process," he replied as he set the dirty plates in the sink.

The remark earned him a sigh. "I know."

"Mommy, Wayne wants a beer," Steffi called out from the dining room table. "And can I have a cookie?"

"Absolutely you can have a cookie, baby. Come on in here and I'll give you one." Reaching into the cabinet, she took down a bag of chocolate frosted cookies and took out two.

"Tell Wayne I said he could get his own drinks," she told the girl after handing the treats over.

"Okay, Mommy."

"Honest to God," Roxanne said after Steffi skipped back into the other room. "Asking a four-year-old to pick him up a drink. What kind of idiot does that?"

Mike waited while Roxanne watched Steffi leave the room. He could sense the wheels turning inside his head. Wayne's sudden appearance had, in a weird way, helped his cause.

"Going to the press," she said. "You really think it'll help?"

"Keep the Sinclairs from burying the case under a mound of legal paperwork."

"And you're sure we can control the message?"

Translation, he was certain they could protect Steffi. "You know what they say. Best defense is a good offense."

"What's the big deal? It's only a beer." Wayne shuffled his way to the fridge, grabbed a can, paused and grabbed a second. "Wasn't like the kid was doing anything."

"Do it," she said as soon as Wayne shuffled back.

Mike tried to keep his enthusiasm at a minimum so he didn't scare her off. "You sure?"

"I'm sure," she said, eyes finding Steffi. "I want to speed this case along."

"Great. I'll start drafting a plan right way. Find a marketing consultant who will be able to help us out." He worked with a good one back at Ashby Gannon. Expensive but good.

Roxanne continued to look off in Steffi's direction. Her hands twisted in the hem of her T-shirt, rolling and unrolling the material. "Hey," he said, catching hold of one. "You made the right call."

The doubt in her eyes as she looked at him stung. "I won't let anything go wrong. I promise."

It frightened him how much he meant his words.

CHAPTER SIX

"Shoot, shoot, shoot."

"Mommy you're saying bad words."

"I know, baby. I'm sorry. Mom's just really late for an appointment." Really, really late.

It was Saturday morning. Last night Mike showed up at the lounge requesting—make that insisting—she show up to his office this morning. Why he couldn't make the request over the phone she didn't know; he seemed to have this thing for coming by her workplace.

For that matter, she didn't know why she had to show up on a Saturday morning. "We need to get you ready for next week's interview," he'd said. Roxy kinda thought she was ready. They'd spent the whole week working with some fancy consultant he knew who liked picking apart how she pronounced words. "Going with a g, not an a, Miss O'Brien. And don't slouch." If it weren't for Mike and his soothing "You're doing great, Roxanne," she'd have walked out.

Doubt there'd be too much praise being tossed around this morning. She was over a half hour late. Nothing had gone right. First she woke to find Wayne and some complete stranger sleeping the night off in her living room. Then Mrs. Ortega called to say she couldn't babysit forcing her to drag Steffi along. Finally, to top it all off, she missed her scheduled bus meaning she had to hike half a block to the subway station. One more lousy piece of luck and she'd lose it.

"I know, I know, I'm late," she said in a rush when she finally found her way into Mike's office. "This morning has been absolutely—"

The most stunning-looking woman Roxy had ever seen sat on the edge of Mike's desk, Jimmy Choo dangling from her toe. She had blond glossy hair that she wore clipped at the base of her neck and the type of lips women spent thousands of dollars in collagen to achieve. Only hers looked natural. She wore a duster-style sweater and camel hair slacks. Another consultant?

If so, she looked mighty at home around Mike.

Roxy shifted Steffi, who she'd scooped up upon leaving the elevator, from one hip to the other. Mike could have at least warned her there'd be someone joining them so she could have worn something a little better than jeans and a turtleneck.

"Finally!" Mike said. "I was concerned something had happened."

His attention went to Steffi. "Or maybe something did. Hello, Steffi."

Steffi stared.

"Babysitting issues," Roxy explained. "Mrs. Ortega canceled. I didn't have anyone else to watch her."

"No worries. Happens to the best of us," the blonde remarked.

Mike gave the woman a look. "Since when did you grow tolerant of child care issues?"

"Since I became a parent."

"You're not a parent. You're a dog owner," Mike replied.

"She's still a responsibility."

"One you can carry in your purse."

The banter was nauseatingly good-humored. If the woman was another consultant, she was one Mike obviously knew very well. It dawned on Roxy that the blonde was exactly the kind of woman she pictured with Mike, too.

She moved with the same kind of fluid grace, rising to her feet and extending a perfectly manicured hand. "Mike's apparently too busy hassling me about my dog to be polite. I'm Sophie Messina," she said. "It's nice to meet you, Roxanne."

"Sophie is here to help you get ready for your public debut," Mike explained.

Get ready, how? She'd already worked with the media guy. Her skepticism started to kick in. Calling upon what few acting skills she had, Roxy pretended a smile. "Really?"

"Don't worry, I won't push you to do anything drastic," the blonde—Sophie—replied. "Alfredo is going to love your hair by the way."

Roxy narrowed her eyes. "Who's Alfredo?"

"You don't know?" Wearing a frown, Sophie spun around to face Mike. "You did tell her what we were doing today, didn't you?"

"I planned to explain once we were all together."

"Explain once—? You're kidding me."

"Explain what?" Roxy looked at the two of them.

Oh, my God. Smooth out the rough edges. That's what he wrote while in the bar that first night. Part of the overall plan, he'd said. He'd share when he was ready.

He'd been talking about *her* rough edges. "This is a makeover?" she asked them.

Why didn't he come right out and say she wasn't suitable for talking to the press? Too "rough" as it were.

"You son of a—" She caught herself before Steffi heard the next word.

"Roxanne, wait."

"For what? For you to insult me more?"

Forget it.

"What do you mean, insult?"

"When you said this was to prepare for next week's interview, I thought you meant working on my interview skills. Not my appearance."

"I told you you should have said something beforehand," Sophie said, leaning against the desk. "If it were me, I'd be mad, too."

"No one asked your opinion, Sophie," Mike snapped.

"Maybe you should because she's right. What's wrong with the way I look? I've been looking this way for thirty years and it's worked for me just fine."

In the back of her mind, she feared her reaction was over the top as usual. But, dammit, he hurt her feelings. How dare he get his blonde friend to clean her up. She'd thought…

Thought he might think she measured up.

"You misunderstand what I'm trying to do," he said.

"Do I? Because the term makeover sounds pretty clear-cut."

Letting out a long breath, Mike jammed his fingers through his hair. In spite of it being Saturday, he wore a tweed jacket over his lamb's wool sweater. More proof of her inadequacy, Roxy supposed, that she underdressed for a weekend meeting. "Sophie, would you mind taking Steffi to the big conference room and showing her the TV set? I need to talk with Roxanne alone."

To her credit, the blonde silently asked permission before moving. Nodding, Roxy set her daughter on the floor and nudged her toward the door. "It's okay, Steffi. I'll be there in a minute."

"I thought you understood how important it is to put your best foot forward when speaking to the press," Mike said after the door shut.

"Oh, I understand." All too well. "Apparently you don't consider my foot good enough."

"Not true. Your foot is fine."

"Just not good enough to show the world."

"Oh, come on, Roxy, use your head. This isn't about whether or not you look good. It's about selling you as Wentworth Sinclair's daughter. You're an actress. Think of this as playing a role. Roxanne O'Brien, heiress."

"I am Roxanne O'Brien, heiress."

"The public will expect you to look different."

"You mean better." Not like Roxanne O'Brien, cocktail waitress. When was plain old Roxy going to be good enough?

"I mean different," Mike repeated. He stepped forward closing the difference between them until it was no more than a few inches. "They are two vastly difference things, and you know it."

Unfortunately the man had a point. To win over the folks uptown, she had to look like she belonged.

"You still should have told me. You know I don't like secrets."

"I know, but if I told you I risked you not showing up.

"Or having a drink dumped in my lap," he added, offering a slow, charm-laden smile. Roxy decided he was taking up far too much of her personal space than normal. The edge of his tweed blazer abutted her rib cage. Every breath he took caused the wool to gently caress her sweater.

"What about your friend?" she asked. "She doesn't mind doing this?"

"Who, Sophie? Are you kidding? I only had to promise my firstborn. Seriously…" He raised a hand when she opened her mouth to say something. "After she was done lecturing me for blowing her and my brother off for dinner this weekend, she jumped right aboard."

His brother. To her surprise, relief circulated through her.

"So," Mike was saying. Was it her imagination or had he moved another step closer? "Are you on board?"

"What about Steffi? I can't very well take her with me, can I?"

"Now that you say it that might be a problem. I hadn't counted on her showing up."

"I don't suppose—" Roxy shook her head. The idea was ludicrous.

"What?" Mike pressed.

"Well, I was wondering if you'd be, well, if you'd watch Steffi. But then I realized what a bad idea that was."

"It's not bad at all," he replied. "I wasn't going to go on this excursion of yours anyway."

"You weren't?"

"Get in the way of two women and shopping? I'm not sure it's worth the risk. I'd be glad to watch Steffi."

"You?" Him? The two barely spoke to one another. What would they do, spend the afternoon staring at each other? She chewed her lower lip. "I'm not sure."

"Trust me," Mike said, his voice transforming soft and silky.

Maybe now would be a good idea to remind him about her theory on promises and the men who made and broke them. Or rather it might have been if Mike hadn't moved close enough she could feel his breath on her neck. "Have I lied to you yet?" he asked.

"I—" Roxy had to think. No, he hadn't. There had been misunderstandings and some poor behavior but he never lied. "You promise to help me keep on top of information," she said. "Good, bad or otherwise. Deal?"

The smile gracing his features was so slow and sexy her knees practically buckled. "Everything," Mike reassured her, and darn if his face wasn't so sincere her stomach tumbled a little. To save herself, she stepped backward.

"All right," she said, "let's get this makeup party started."

"Believe me, I had no idea Mike planned to spring today on you like this," Sophie said a short while later. "I thought for sure he'd explain himself. I swear sometimes he's worse than his brother. Grant lives to keep me off balance."

Roxy listened, but didn't answer. She still wasn't happy about this whole makeover project, even if she could see Mike's point. Partly out of anger, partly because she had no idea what the end product would look like.

"I have to admit, though," the blond woman continued, "it was fun watching you give him the what-for."

She held a silver-and-white jacket next to Roxy's face, then shook her head. "You ask me, he needs someone to do that more often. Might loosen him up a little—the man makes me look low-key." A stretch since the woman had already checked her email a dozen times since leaving the office. "Lord knows Grant's been trying to get him to loosen that tie of his for a while."

"I like how formal he looks," Roxy replied.

"No wonder he likes you."

Roxy hated how her stomach somersaulted at Sophie's comment. Same way she hated trying not to relive the moment in his office or any of the other times he'd come close to touching her. Reminding herself theirs was a temporary relationship helped. "Winning this case seems to be important to him."

"Winning, huh?" A pair of skeptical blue eyes stared at her from over the clothes rack. "That why he practically leaped over his desk when you walked in the door? And offered to watch your daughter while we shopped?"

Another flutter found its way to Roxy's stomach. "He probably figured we'd get more done without having to entertain a four-year-old."

"If you say so."

Roxy said so. For once she planned to use her head rather than blindly acting out. She shook her head at the cashmere blazer Sophie had held up. "Too high a cost."

"Sometimes you need to break out of your comfort mold," Sophie replied. "Grant taught me that. In this case, you might find this to be a good investment."

They were talking about the jacket, right?

"I have to admit," Sophie continued. "I've never seen Mike so invested in a case before. Or maybe it seems that way because we haven't seen him much. He's too busy building his super firm."

"Super firm?" Roxy had to ask.

"It's what we prefer to call it because he's always out drumming up business. Grant figures he's on a quest to create the biggest, bestest law firm in the city. That would certainly make my future in-laws happy."

Least you have a choice. "Mike mentioned being from a family of high achievers."

"You can say that again." Turning around from the rack to the shelves behind her, Sophie began looking through a collection of turtleneck sweaters. "Normally I would agree with the philosophy."

"But?" Roxy heard the unspoken word quite clearly.

The blonde shrugged. "Something about the Templetons. They demand a lot of their kids, even as adults. But what do I know? My parents didn't demand a damn thing from me."

"Me, neither."

"I knew I liked you for some reason," Sophie said with a grin.

As Roxy fingered the leather piping that trimmed a red blazer, a sadness settled over her. *Least you had the choice.* Mike's remark kept coming back to her. Was this the nerve she kept hitting with her questions about his family? The one that made him fold into himself whenever the topic came up?

"Funny," Sophie said. "I expected more clutter."

"Where?" Her remark brought Roxy back to the present.

"At Mike's firm. Today was the first time I visited. I was surprised how little clutter there was. My firm went paperless a while back, and we're still buried in the stuff."

"You're surprised Mike is neat?" Picturing her formal-looking attorney, she couldn't imagine anything about him being cluttered.

"Mike, no. The rest of the staff, yes, I mean, I know it's a co-op office space and they share resources, but he must have at least one paralegal or secretary. I can't believe he managed to find one as neat as he is."

She touched Roxy's shoulder. "Ready to try a few outfits on? I can't wait to see how the wrap dress fits. I have a feeling Mike's eyes will bug out of his head when he sees you in it."

Roxy looked to the ground. The remark was meant to be a compliment. Too bad she didn't feel flattered. It only reminded her she was here because Mike thought she needed "smoothing."

"I thought the point was to impress the Sinclairs," she said.

"It is," Sophie replied. "But would it hurt to impress your lawyer, too?"

"No." She only wished she'd been impressive enough from the start.

My Dearest Fiona:
I miss you, too. When you're not with me, it feels as though the life has been sucked right out of the room. You're my sunshine, my light. Outside my window, I can see the last few leaves of fall. A living O. Henry painting. Their color is nothing compared to yours. Because without you the world feels dead. When I get home, I'm going to take you in my arms and...

Nice dream, pal. Mike set Wentworth's letter down. It was the next to last one in the pile. Twenty-eight letters in looking for information that might prove Wentworth and Fiona fathered a child and he hadn't unearthed a thing. Nothing but a rapidly growing unsettled feeling. Almost like a yearning. And memories of his own college affair. One semester. He'd crammed a lifetime in, though, hadn't he? Enough, he'd assumed, to last.

Odd thing was, it wasn't those days or even those people he missed. Grace, for all the feelings she evoked in him, wasn't what had him feeling empty. It was more. A large, indefinable emotion that he couldn't escape. Same way he couldn't shake how whenever he thought of those days now, Grace's fuzzy dark-haired image morphed into a less fuzzy, decided red-haired one.

"You tap your pen a lot."

At the far end of the conference table, Steffi sat munching on carrot slices. She was staring at him with those big eyes of hers.

"Nervous habit," he answered.

"Why are you nervous?"

"I'm wondering why your mom and Sophie aren't back yet, is all." The pair had been gone for almost four hours. What was taking so long? Making matters worse, Sophie refused to answer his last two texts. "You'll have to wait and see" she'd written before signing off.

"Are they lost?" Steffi's eyes got wide and her lower lip started to jut out.

Great. He didn't mean to make the girl worry. "No, no, nothing like that. When I say nervous I mean eager."

"What's eager?"

You dug yourself into a hole on that one. Mike set down his pen. "Eager is a good thing. It means I'm looking forward to seeing your mother again."

"Because you miss her?"

Talk about a loaded question. "Because she was going shopping, and I want to see what she bought."

He was beginning to wonder if asking Sophie to help had been a good idea. Along with having expensive tastes, his brother's girlfriend was used to talking charge. Combine her control freakiness with Roxanne's quick temper and you were talking incendiary. Visions of two strong-willed women coming to verbal blows popped into his head. Wouldn't that be an excellent headline? Would-Be Heiress Throws Left Hook in Salon.

If he wanted to be brutally honest with himself, the more pressing reason he wanted to talk with Roxanne was to make sure she'd truly forgiven him. It wasn't as if he truly meant to keep his plans a secret. He'd merely been concerned how she would react to his suggestion. He figured if he waited till the last minute, the process would go smoother. A bad plan, as it turned out.

Then again, when it came to Roxy, he seemed to travel down Bad Plan road a lot. If he was going to make this so-called media tour work, he needed to remember to keep his priorities straight.

"I miss Mommy," Steffi said as she stuffed a carrot slice in her mouth. "I don't like it when I have babysitters."

"You don't like the lady who watches you?"

He'd just gotten burned by a four-year-old. "Mrs. Ortega smells like cold medicine."

Lucky Mrs. Ortega. Wonder what the girl thought of him.

"I'm sure your mom will be back soon. I know she doesn't like to leave you with babysitters longer than she has to." He got a warm feeling thinking about Roxy's dedication. One of many things he was starting to appreciate. Along with her green eyes and shapely behind and the vulnerability that never seemed far from her surface.

"You like Mommy?"

Steffi's question startled him. How'd the little dickens manage to read his thoughts?

His answer, he realized, had to be well thought out. He didn't want to give the girl the wrong impression. Finally he decided on the very benign. "Your mother is a very nice woman."

"Wayne says she's stuck up."

Wayne was a jerk. He could tell from their first meeting. "Do you think Mommy's stuck up?"

"What?" If he'd been drinking he'd have choked. "No. I don't think she's stuck up at all."

"'Cause you like her?"

Mike sighed. Like Roxanne? Hell, yeah, he liked her. Way too much. "It's complicated," he told the little girl.

Wrong answer.

"What's complicated?" she immediately asked.

"Complicated means hard." For crying out loud, how many more questions was this little girl going to ask? She was worse than opposing counsel. "Do you need more juice?"

She didn't fall for his diversion attempt. "Why is it hard?"

Because she's my client. Because there are rules and ethical considerations. Because she wasn't part of the plan. He had a whole list of reasons, none of which would make sense to a girl her age. Hell, at the moment none of them made sense to him. "Your mommy and I are friends," he told her.

"Oh." Whether she found the answer satisfying or disappointing, Mike couldn't tell. Her attention had returned to the plastic bag of carrots and the hair tumbling in front of her face that rendered her expression invisible. He should be relieved she was no longer asking difficult questions, only he wasn't. He felt bad she'd grown so quiet.

Looking up, he swore the second hand had gone

backward. In a few minutes, she would be done with her snack and then what? More television? There wasn't anything on to interest her. He knew because she'd already made that pronouncement before getting out her snack. Too bad she couldn't read well yet. He'd teach her to file.

A spotted white-and-purple pony caught his eye, giving him an idea. *Thank you, Dusty.*

"Did you know there's a merry-go-round carousel a few blocks from here?"

Steffi's jaw dropped midchew. She was staring again. "You interested in going?" he asked.

A spark of excitement lit up her face, but she still didn't answer. At some point Roxy probably told her to never go anywhere without Roxy's permission and he could see that her four-year-old brain was trying to determine a loophole. Her pensive expression looked so much like her mother's he felt a tug in his chest.

Things were definitely becoming complicated if a child's expression could affect him.

Before a decision could be made, they heard the sound of female laughter coming from the hallway.

"Mommy's back!" Steffi jumped from her seat and ran toward the door. Mike followed behind. At this point, he wasn't sure who was happier to see them return. That is, he was eager to see how his investment paid off.

The main office door opened and wow! Mike had to grab hold of the reception desk to keep his balance. The woman walking through the door with Sophie was… Was…

He'd lost his ability to speak. It was as if Alfredo and Sophie had conspired to take Roxy's natural beauty and softness and shove them under a magnifying glass. Her red mane had been tamed into thick, strawberry-blond locks that tumbled about her shoulders. The skinny jeans and sweater were gone, too. Tossed in favor of a black-and-white wraparound dress and cardigan sweater that subtly showed off her curves. The hint of flesh dipping to a V between her breasts was as enticing as any low-cut camisole. And her legs… Discreetly he stole a look at her bottom half.

"You look different, Mommy," Steffi said.

"Think so?" Roxy asked.

"Uh-huh. Your hair is straight."

Her eyes found his, looking for his reaction. Had her skin always looked this luminescent or was it the expertly applied makeup? "You look amazing," he replied.

"Then I guess the transformation is complete."

A shadow flickered across her face, and had he been less distracted, he might have questioned what it meant. As it was, though, he was too busy absorbing the change.

Other than the straight hair and different clothes, she didn't look *drastically* different. Not when he had a chance to study her. It was like everything good and attractive about her appearance had been given a polish. Gone was the fatigue, in favor of brighter cheeks and eyes. She looked…softer, less worn down. The way she was meant to look had life not kicked her around.

"Exactly how an heiress should look," he said softly. How she deserved to look.

Her lashes were thick half-moons as she looked down. "Thank you." There was an odd tone to her voice he couldn't quite place. But then, his listening skills had taken a backseat in favor of other senses.

Somewhere in the background, a throat cleared.

Finding his senses, Mike looked to Sophie who had positioned herself against the coat closet door, arms folded, like a proud artist displaying her work. "Thank you for your help," he said.

"My pleasure. It was fun having someone to shop with for a change. I was right about Alfredo, too. Soon as he saw her hair, he was in heaven. What'd he call you, his 'Strawberry-haired goddess'?"

Roxanne's voice was no more than a notch above a whisper. "Something like that."

"He never gushes over me like that," Sophie said. "He loved her. Absolutely loved her."

Who wouldn't, Mike caught himself thinking.

"More likely he loved the check you wrote at the end of the appointment." With a smile, Roxanne squatted down so she was eye to eye with Steffi. Not for the first time, Mike was impressed by the way she lit up when talking to the little girl. It was obvious to anyone watching Steffi meant everything to her mother.

"We bought you a present, too." She handed the little girl a pink polka-dotted gift bag, which Steffi immediately dived into.

Her responding squeal could be heard across the street. "It's a pony sweater!" She held up the purple knit top.

"I thought he looked like Dusty. Don't worry, I paid for it myself," she said to Mike. "So it won't get mixed in with your business expenses."

"I wouldn't have minded," he replied, surprised at how much he meant the statement. He watched Steffi struggling to pull the sweater over her head and decided, again to his surprise, that her enthusiasm would have been worth the cost.

"Would you like some help with that?" Sophie asked. "There's a mirror in the ladies' room so you can see what you look like."

"I'll take her," Roxy said.

"No, you stay and finish your conversation with Mike. The two of us will be fine." Sophie rescued both the sweater and the girl and took her by the hand. "So you like horses?" she asked as she led her away.

"Uh-huh." Steffi chattered all the way to the door and into the hall, where the door shut behind her, muffling her running commentary.

"Guess she liked the sweater," Roxy said as she watched her go.

Something was off, Mike realized all of a sudden. A note missing from her voice. A light from her eyes. No sooner did Steffi disappear behind closed doors than the one illuminating her faded. "What is it?" he heard himself ask.

"Nothing important. Did the two of you have a good afternoon?"

He thought about his and Steffi's conversation. "We survived. I learned she doesn't like her baby-sitters." As he held out a hand and helped her back to her feet, he explained what she had said about Mrs. Ortega.

"Arthritis rub," Roxy replied. "Has a lot of menthol. Makes for a pretty pungent smell."

"Hopefully she doesn't have an equally distasteful description of my aroma."

"Doubt it. You smell pretty good."

Not as good as you, he said to himself. Seduced

by the new Roxanne, he leaned farther into her space and breathed deep. Thank God the make-over process hadn't erased the uniqueness of her scent. Underneath the hair spray, he could still detect the faint odor he found intoxicating. Suddenly the office felt very empty. He still had his hand resting beneath her elbow. Quickly he removed it, fingers tensing in revolt. They wanted to stay in contact, tighten their grip even, and pull her closer.

"I can't get over how different you look," he said.

Emotion passed across her face, unreadable and uncertain. "Different good or different bad?"

Her real question was unspoken, but he understood just the same. As if she could ever look bad, he wanted to say. "Different," he said instead, hoping his failure to deliver a solid verdict would make his point. He scanned her face. "I think it's the lack of curls. I miss them."

"You do?" She looked surprised.

"Yeah." There had been an untamed quality to her curls that appealed to him. This look was far more reined in, far more controlled. He caught a strand between his thumb and index finger, the back of his hand brushing her temple as he did so. Her sharp intake of breath was unmistakable. Searching her face, he saw her eyes were shifting from hazel to dark green. That was one thing the makeover could never change. The ever-changing color of her gaze. So damn gorgeous.

"Mommy! Mommy! I love my new sweater!"

At the sound of Steffi's voice, both of them stepped backward, breaking the closeness and the moment. Though, not before Mike swore he saw another shadow crossing Roxanne's face.

The little girl raced up to them, Sophie trailing behind. "Whoa! Slow down so I can see if it fits," Roxanne said. Immediately the four-year-old skidded to a stop, a reverse one-eighty in speed.

"She's very excited," Sophie said, stating the obvious. Watching her rush to regain control was kind of amusing. Sophie was nothing, if not order obsessed.

"Can I wear my sweater when we go to the library?" Steffi asked. Having endured her mother's inspection, she was, at the moment, spinning airplane circles.

"The library?"

Steffi stopped her running. "To see the carousel," Steffi replied. If four-year-olds were capable of verbal eye rolls, Steffi had just accomplished one. She stated the destination as if it was a fact out of *Encyclopedia Britannica* and they were all foolish for forgetting. "Mike said we could go."

"Did he now?"

"You're kidding me," Sophie drawled.

Roxy looked over, the surprise causing the green in her eyes to deepen. Heated discomfort rolled through him. He grabbed hold of the reception desk again, pretending to lean. "I may have mentioned the carousel in Bryant Park. I told her we could take a ride over there," he said to Sophie.

"Can I wear my sweater?" Steffi asked. "Please, please!"

"Wait," Sophie interrupted. "You were going to go ride a merry-go-round? You."

He should have known Sophie would have a comment. "No need to sound so surprised. It's a nice day...the kid's been cooped up in my office. Why not take her for some fresh air?"

"Because you don't..." She waved off the sentence, going for her handbag instead. "I've got to call Grant. He won't believe this."

Triumphantly she brandished her cell phone before casting a smile in Roxanne's direction. "I'd take him up on it. Who knows when he'll make an offer like this again."

Sophie was a fine one to talk. She probably emptied her in-box while waiting at the salon. In reality, he'd forgotten his offer the second Roxanne returned, but now that Steffi reminded him, the afternoon didn't sound all that awful.

From her expression, Roxy didn't share his enthusiasm. "I don't know, baby," she started to say. "It's getting late and—"

"*Pul-leeze*. One ride?"

"I did promise," Mike said, figuring that would push the odds in his favor.

He figured right. The woman was a pushover in terms of her daughter. "All right," she said, adding a sigh to show she wasn't completely one hundred percent on board. "We'll go. But only one ride. Then we head home."

"Yay!" Steffi clasped her hands.

From his spot near the reception desk, Mike smiled at the mother and daughter team. He wasn't sure if he'd stepped back on Bad Idea road or not, but watching the two of them smiling, he couldn't help feeling like he'd just had a major win.

Now if he could only figure out what the shadow that kept showing up on Roxanne's face meant.

CHAPTER SEVEN

"MERRY-GO-ROUND, merry-go-round."

Steffi singsonged the words under her breath as they waited in line at the ticket stand. Her body bounced with excitement.

Roxy was happy for her. She loved watching her daughter having a good time. She just couldn't believe it was at Mike Templeton's suggestion.

"You really planned to take her here on your own?"

Maybe it was the unseasonably warm weather but the park was crowded with families, in spite it being off-season. Some waited in line to ride the custom-made carousel while more milled around a makeshift stage waiting for the next public event. A sign told people Frogiere the French Frog would be arriving in an hour. Several children carried picture books bearing the same name.

"I admit, I wasn't expecting the park to be this crowded," he replied. "It's a good thing you arrived when you did to save us."

Roxy pretended not to catch his grin. She was still annoyed with him over the whole makeover business. Although taking Steffi to a carousel did thaw her a little.

A hand brushed the back of her legs. Looking over her shoulder, she saw a boy a couple years younger than Steffi weaving his way around his mother's legs letting his fingers drift across everything within reach.

The woman immediately apologized. Roxy saw she was wearing a sweater similar to Sophie's, and sported a loudly large diamond. A second child, a little girl, held her right hand and stole looks at Steffi. Both children looked impeccable.

Self-consciousness washed over her from head to toe. "It's all right," she said. "No harm done."

"That's because we washed off the ice cream before getting in line," the woman said smiling. "This is your daughter's first time on the carousel?"

"Yes, it is."

"Jacob's, too. Though, I try to take Samantha once a month when the weather is decent."

The two women began chatting about entertaining children during the winter. Maybe it was her imagination, but Roxy had to ask herself whether the woman would have chatted with her had she been wearing her old clothes. Possibly not. Certainly felt to her she'd been treated differently since the makeover. People who would never speak to her or show her the slightest bit of deference seemed to be extra friendly all of a sudden.

She wished she knew how she felt about the whole thing.

On one hand, when she first looked in the mirror after Alfredo worked his magic, as he put it, she'd loved what she saw. The woman in the reflection looked sleek and sophisticated. A second later, she grew upset with herself. Wasn't approving of her new look a betrayal? A passive agreement that Mike had been right—she needed smoothing out?

Then there was Mike himself. She definitely didn't imagine his expression when she returned to his office. He hadn't been able to take his eyes off her. And when his hand brushed her skin… Even the memory caused excitement and she absent-mindedly pressed a fist to her stomach to prevent the emotion from taking hold. Disappointment quickly followed in its tracks anyway. Because Mike's attraction was for the made-over Roxy. It wasn't any more real or substantive than the makeup and clothes.

What killed her the most was how happy she'd been at his reaction, no matter what the reason.

She was becoming way too attached to the man's approval for her own good.

"You're so lucky your husband is willing to go with you. Mine is busy with paperwork."

Roxy whipped her head toward Mike. "Oh, he's not—"

"Making this a regular visit?" Mike answered. "You're right. Did you see those ticket prices? Highway robbery."

"The things we do for our kids, huh?" the woman remarked.

He was reaching into his back pocket for his wallet, but his attention had dropped to the bouncing Steffi. "You can say that again."

He couldn't say it once. Steffi wasn't his kid. "Why did you let that woman think we were married?" Roxy asked once they'd moved from the ticket line to the carousel line.

"Why not? Easier than launching into a long explanation about our relationship."

That was just it. They didn't have a relationship beyond lawyer and client. His pretending otherwise was just another layer of fantasy on a day thick with it.

Though smaller than the one in Central Park, the Bryant Park carousel was bright and cheery with beautiful hand-carved animals. Roxy spotted not only horses but a tiger and a whimsical white rabbit. The sounds of foreign music could be barely made out over the noise of kids and conversation. A sign on the fence said that the song was in French, and that the carousel was based on one in France. Roxy looked around the crowd. Her ticket line acquaintance with her two children were a few people back. She pushed an empty double stroller while her kids were creeping along the barrier fence, something Steffi and half the other kids were doing as well. The mother saw her and offered a commiserating shrug. In front of her, there was a pair of teenage mothers dressed decidedly non-motherly with their children balanced on their hips. Roxy smiled hello, but got nothing but cold blank stares in return.

A few yards from the gate, Steffi squealed in excitement. "Look! It's Dusty!"

Not quite, but there was a brilliant white horse with gold and red trim. "I want to ride him!"

"You'll have to wait and see, baby. There are other kids in line, too. Someone else might get on him first."

As she pretty much expected, her warning fell on deaf ears. Steffi was too busy showing Dusty his "twin." "Dusty wants to ride him, too." She grinned and held the pony over her head for a better look.

Their turn came and the crowd filed onto the

wooden platform, where the other kids immediately started running to snag their favorite animal. Steffi was no different. She took off like a shot for her treasured white stallion only to be beat out by a boy in a green puffy coat.

Instantly her daughter's lower lip jutted out. "Sorry, baby. Let's see if there's another horse." Though she would certainly live with the disappointment, Roxy knew Steffi would be let down if she had to ride a different animal or, heaven forbid, one of the sleighs with bench seats. Unfortunately, as they made their way around the circle, it looked more and more like that would be the case.

Nice to see the new look hadn't changed everything.

"Look!" Steffi pulled at her arm, practically removing it from its socket as they rounded the first turn. Soon enough Roxy saw why, and when she did, her chest grew too full for her body. There stood Mike in all his tweeded splendor, leaning against a second white pony. "I saw there was a mate, and figured while you tried to snag the first one, I'd lock in a backup."

It was stupid, but Roxy wanted to throw her arms around him. "Will this pony work?" she asked Steffi.

The little girl nodded, and Roxy moved to lift her up. "You have to hold on with both hands," she said. "Dusty will have to ride with us, okay?" She put her hand out ready to collect the precious plastic horse.

That's when it happened.

The little girl turned to Mike and held out the toy. The lawyer looked like he'd been struck. He stared at the toy for a couple seconds before gently wrapping his long fingers around its plastic middle. "I'll let him ride with me, okay?"

Her daughter nodded.

The fullness in Roxy's chest tripled. Such a simple exchange, and it made her heart ache. The merry-go-round resumed with a jerk, the calliope playing loudly in the center. She barely heard. Nor did she notice the noise and families crowding around her. All her attention was focused on the man and little girl in her orbit. Standing on this wooden platform, she found herself wishing the fantasy could continue. That Saturday afternoons in the park with carousels and giant story-reading frogs was the norm. Not barroom drunks or Wayne passed out in her living room.

Of course, Mike would tell her that once the Sinclairs recognized her existence, this could be her regular life. She could spoil Steffi rotten with merry-go-rounds and ponies and all the giant frogs she wanted.

Only one problem. She wasn't sure that even

then the fantasy would be complete. She had a very bad feeling it could never be complete without a certain tweed-wearing ingredient. But he'll have moved on. To the next case, the next challenge. Why wouldn't he? Underneath it all, she'd still be the same old Roxy. He thought her lacking before; eventually the gloss would wear off and he'd find her lacking again.

When the ride was over and Frogiere had made his appearance, they headed to a small café at the rear of the library. Roxy gazed out over the space and the people milling about. "Twenty-nine years living in New York, and not once have I been in this park. Closest I ever came was walking past it on my way to an audition."

"Don't feel bad. It's my first time, too. Too much else going on during the weekends," he added.

Horseback riding, swimming and all those other accomplishments. How could she forget?

"Though now that I think about it," he said, frowning, "the carousel might not have been here when I was really little. I don't remember. I'll have to ask Grant."

"Oh, that reminds me. Sophie said to tell you this is the last time you're allowed to cancel plans."

After checking over at Steffi, who was engrossed in playing with Dusty, Roxy continued,

"She's nice. I feel bad for acting like such a brat in front of her." Rightful reason or not, she had to rein in her reactions.

"I wouldn't worry too much. From the tirade I received from her, she considers everything my fault anyway. She doesn't mince words, that's for certain. Probably why Grant likes her so much."

Which reminded her of another comment she was supposed to pass on. "She also thinks the reason you're avoiding the two of them so much is that you feel like the odd man out."

Mike flipped over his menu. "When did she say that to you?"

"At the salon."

"Well, she's being ridiculous."

"Was she?" Then why was he hiding behind his menu while answering? And he was hiding because he wasn't wearing his glasses and therefore couldn't read the type.

"I couldn't be happier for her and Grant. She's good for him. Really good."

"Then why do you keep canceling?"

"I've been busy," he replied, flipping the two-page menu back to its top page. "I've got a law firm to attend to."

The megafirm Grant thought he was trying to build up. The one without clutter, as Sophie put it. Then again, who was she to judge what an office was supposed to look like? "Are you glad you opened your own practice?"

He set the menu down. "What makes you ask?" His tone was harsher than she expected. Way more than the question warranted.

"No real reason. I've been thinking about choices lately is all. The ones my mother made, the ones I made, and wondered, seeing all the time you have to work at it, if you're sorry you didn't stay at your old firm." She wondered even more now, following his reaction.

Mike sipped his water. He retrieved a fork Steffi dropped on the ground. He placed their orders with the waitress. The one thing he didn't do was give her an answer. When the waitress was gone and he leaned forward in his chair, Roxy thought he might but he asked, "Do you regret quitting acting?"

Was this answering a question with a question some kind of tactic or simply changing the topic?

"Wasn't like I had much to give up." One of them should answer. "Kind of like asking a punching bag if he misses getting hit."

"Couldn't have been so bad."

"I once got told I was too stiff to point at tile samples in a cable access commercial. Trust me, when I say I was terrible, I was terrible."

"Then why...?"

"Did I try?" She shrugged. "I loved pretending to be someone else." Sort of what you're doing now, a voice in her head said. Ignoring it, she reached over and brushed the curls from Steffi's eyes. "I like to think I ended up with the better end of the bargain, although sometimes I wonder if the next audition would have been *the* audition. The one that pushed me into the big-time. It would have been awesome seeing my name in lights."

Their conversation was interrupted by the waitress bringing their order and Steffi expressing wonder at the slab of chocolate cake put in front of her. Roxy immediately earned a brief pout by cutting the piece into two uneven pieces.

"Success isn't all it's cracked up to be," Mike said once the waitress was out of earshot. "It comes with responsibility." His eyes faded a million miles away. "You're expected to always measure up, be an example to others." His finger traced the rim of his glasses. Sad, deliberate circles. "It's not as easy as it looks."

"You've done all right so far."

So far. His tone was hollow. Was he trying to tell her that while not knowing failure, Mike's life had had costs? What kind? she wondered. How deep did the marks go?

"Do you have regrets?"

He didn't answer right away, automatically giving her what she wanted to know. "Regret implies having a choice."

A cop-out answer. Well acquainted with them she recognized the dodge immediately. Never dodge a dodger. There was regret, the evidence lay in the nerve she so consistently pushed whenever she mentioned his family.

She decided to take a chance and push for more. "Who was she?"

"Who?"

"Your regret. I'm guessing it's either a person or a career choice, and since you said you always wanted to be a lawyer…"

Actually if she remembered, he said he couldn't remember a time when he wasn't planning to be a lawyer, but wording wasn't important. Her shot in the dark worked. "Neither," he replied. "Or maybe the answer would be both."

He carved off a piece of apple tart. "Spring of my junior year my adviser told me I was short humanities credits. The number fell through the cracks while I was trying to get in all my major coursework. Anyway, since it was late in the registration process, the only class I could fit in my schedule was philosophy. I had to spend twelve weeks arguing the meaning of life and existentialism."

"Somehow I have trouble picturing you." Steffi

carved a bite off her cake and waited for more. Was his regret that he had to take the class?

Apparently not. "Best semester of my life," he told her. "Our study group used to meet Thursday nights at this dive of a bar on the edge of campus where we'd go for hours, and on weekends we'd crash at one of the member's off campus apartment. Grace Reynolds was her name."

Hearing the wistfulness in his voice, Roxy felt a pang of jealousy. Clearly Grace was the female part of the regret.

"We were going to spend the summer backpacking around Europe—our grand scheme to study political cultures up close. You wouldn't have recognized me."

Based on the man he just described, Roxy agreed. The life was so far removed from the starched, formal man she'd come to know. "What happened?"

"My parents arrived with word I'd gotten an internship at Ashby Gannon. Backpacking or career." He shrugged and reached for a sugar packet. "I chose career."

But had he wanted to? He was trying to act as if the answer was a given, but she wasn't so sure. "What happened with Grace?" Of all the questions she had, the aftermath of his love affair came out first. She needed to know.

"Pretty much what you'd expect. She went backpacking—I went to work. When I returned to school in the fall she was living with someone else. I was studying for the LSATs. We both moved on with our lives."

But the price had been paid, hadn't it? No wonder she'd felt such a connection that day in his office. She was sensing the loneliness he kept so very carefully hidden. Her chest once again squeezed with emotion. Its force scared the hell out of her and called her closer at the same time.

Ever since she'd hired Mike Templeton, she'd sworn she'd use her head instead of her heart. Heaven help her, doing so just got a lot harder.

It was three hours later when the taxicab pulled in front of her building, and Mike climbed out with a sleepy Steffi propped against his shoulder.

After Bryant Park, they'd gone back to Mike's office where Roxy practiced interview questions.

"You didn't have to ride all the way here with us," she told him when they reached her front door. She would have been content with saying goodbye at the office, but Mike insisted.

"Didn't feel right. You had your hands pretty full." He tipped his head toward the packages draped over his wrist along with Steffi, whose legs were wrapped tightly around his chest.

"But now my hands are empty."

"Good. Then you can fish your key out faster. This little pony is getting heavy."

"I'm not a pony, I'm a girl," Steffi muttered.

A tired girl at that. Fresh air and excitement had worn her out. She would be asleep before her head hit the pillow.

Roxy unlocked the door and pushed open the glass with her foot. The greeting smell of greasy food told her she was back in her world. "I'll take her from here," she told Mike.

"I don't mind carrying her upstairs."

"I know, but your cab's waiting, and if you don't get back, the driver's likely to leave. I don't want you stuck standing on the street corner."

She reached out and lifted Steffi from his arms. The little girl's body was warm with his body heat. Roxy shivered a little at the sudden onslaught.

"Thanks again for the merry-go-round. Steffi had a fantastic time."

He leaned in, his breath cool and welcome against her cheek. "How about her mother? Did she enjoy herself?"

Roxy smiled. "Yeah, she did."

"Good. Especially since it appears I hurt her feelings this morning."

"Let's forget this morning happened." She didn't want to think about shortcomings, or makeovers or what any of it meant. Not after such a wonderful afternoon. She wanted to keep the fantasy going a little longer.

"Consider it forgotten." He stayed in her space, eyes veiled and searching. Dark half-moons marked his cheeks, shadows caused by the security light shining down on his lashes. Roxy watched as his tongue wet his lower lip, leaving a trail of shine. Those same lips opened as though to speak, and for a moment, her heart stopped, thinking it might not be conversation he wanted.

"See you Monday," he whispered. He meant for her interview, but with his breath on her skin and his hand squeezing hers, the words sounded like a promise of more.

"Monday," she repeated.

She watched him wait by the taxi door while she waited for the elevator, indulging in the contentment his concern created.

"Look at you," Alexis said when she and Steffi walked through the door.

Her roommate sat on the couch watching television, wedged between Wayne, of course, and some large Irish-looking guy she didn't recognize. Both men followed her directions with slow, leering looks that turned Roxy's stomach.

"Whatcha do?" her roomate asked. "Rob a store on Fifth Avenue?"

"Yeah. I thought you said you didn't get any money yet," Wayne added.

"It's part of Mike's strategy. For when I talk to the press. He wanted me to look more like an 'heiress.'"

"He bought you all this?" Alexis had wriggled her way out of the space and made her way to the shopping bags Roxy set down on the chair. "There's a ton of clothes in here. I can't even afford to walk by this store. Wish I had me a lawyer."

"Only way you're getting a lawyer is if that fat butt of yours gets arrested," Wayne shot at her. He cocked another leering smile in Roxy's direction. "So what you have to do to pay him back?"

"Nothing. It's a business expense."

He raised a beer can to his lips. "Uh-huh."

"Mike likes Mommy," Steffi chose that moment to volunteer.

"I bet he does, kid," Wayne replied, elbowing his friend. They both snickered.

Roxy wasn't in the mood. Because she'd spent the day with a gentleman, Wayne's antics were more repulsive to her than ever. Just the sound of his voice made her skin crawl.

She also needed to correct her daughter before impressions got out of hand. "Mike and I are working together, baby. Remember all the practicing we did back in his office?"

Again, Wayne and his friend sniggered.

"For when Mommy has her big meeting Monday," she finished pointedly. All these comments were turning what had been a wonderful day into something cheap and dirty sounding.

"What big meeting?" Alexis asked. She was holding a pale blue turtleneck to her chest, as if she had a hope of fitting her frame into it.

"Mike has a friend who writes for the *Daily Press*. She's going to write a story about me."

"That mean you're getting your money soon?"

"I don't know," Roxy replied. Her roommate didn't need to know the interview was supposed to speed up the process.

"I hope it's soon." Setting the turtleneck down, Alexis began rummaging through another bag. "I'm sick of this dump. Hey, next time you go shopping, you got to take me with you. I want to see if they got anything I would wear."

Roxy's insides stilled. It never dawned on her Alexis planned on moving *with* her. They'd never once discussed plans like that. She'd always assumed the move would be her and Steffi. She never stopped to think Alexis would consider herself part of the plan—or one of the beneficiaries of her inheritance.

"I told you," she said, not sure what else she

could say, "the clothes were a business expense. I won't be going back."

"Oh." There was no disguising the disappointment in her roommate's voice.

"Ha, ha," Wayne said. "Looks like you're out of luck, sis."

The stranger on her couch finally spoke. "I didn't come here to sit around all night talking to your snotty roommate. We gonna party or what?"

"Mama, he said—"

Roxy cut her daughter off. "I know, baby. Just ignore him."

"Yeah, kid. Just ignore us," Wayne said. He was already on his feet and stretching, T-shirt rising up to show his scrawny white stomach. "You comin', Alexis?"

"PJ's friend's throwing an afterhours party on his roof. You wanna join us?"

PJ, she assumed, was the stranger, and he looked less than thrilled at the idea. *Don't worry, pal. Even if I didn't have a kid, I wouldn't join you.* She nodded toward Steffi.

"Oh, yeah, right. Forgot," Alexis replied. "Later then."

"Yeah, later."

Wayne's voice sounded from behind her. "You know, I buy my women things, too, if you're interested."

"Not in your dreams." She flinched as his hot breath dampened her skin. Disgust ran down her spine and turned her stomach.

He replied by muttering one of the vilest words she'd ever heard.

And just like that, the fantasy of the day disappeared, and she found herself back in reality.

Mike's cell phone buzzed the second the cab door closed. Grant had been calling him all night. He'd been told about the carousel from Sophie and eager to give him a hard time, no doubt. He'd probably keep calling all night.

He fished the phone from his pocket and immediately his insides knotted when he saw the caller ID. "Hi, Dad," he greeted. "You're back in the country. How was your trip?"

A few months ago, his mother had been bitten by the urge to see France and dragged his father on a bucket list tour of the country. Naturally, being his parents, they couldn't simply play tourist and they ended up investing in a vineyard they discovered in Bordeaux. They recently went back to check on their investment.

"Terrific. Looks like the initial batch will be top-notch. They're talking about possible medals at the upcoming festivals."

Of course they were. His parents wouldn't invest in anything less than a winning project.

"And you should see your mother. While we were over there, she made friends with one of the local shopkeepers. The woman's teaching her French cooking. I swear, she's going to be the Julia Child of pastry before we're finished. She's gotten so good we've had to take up running to keep the extra pounds off."

Again, not a surprise. They'd probably be doing triathlons next. Cosponsored by their vineyard and the bakery his mother would no doubt start.

"How are things going with you?"

The dreaded question. "Terrific." The lie flowed off his tongue so easily no one would ever guess his stomach had knotted a second time. "I took on a new case last week. Very exciting."

"I know." He did? "I ran into Jim Brassard at Troika yesterday afternoon. He told me you're representing some woman who's going after the Sinclairs?"

Roxy was right. The phrase was unattractive. "I didn't know you and Jim were friends."

"The Bar Association's a small world, Michael. You know that. Is it true?"

"I represent a client with a claim to the estate, if that's what you mean," he replied, not liking the way he referred to Roxanne as some woman.

"Isn't that a little out of character? Since when do you take on flashy cases?"

You think this is flashy, wait till the press interviews start hitting. "I've always handled estate cases. Haven't you always said it takes all kinds to build a practice?"

"Within reason. I also taught you to adhere to some standards. Please tell me I don't have to worry about you passing your business card out at accidents."

Because he was raised better. Mike rolled his eyes. "This is a good case. The woman has a viable claim."

"I hope so. Don't let us down, Michael. Remember, your reputation doesn't just reflect on you in the legal community. You bear my name."

And, as his namesake, had an obligation to not only uphold the Templeton tradition but surpass it. Mike heard the lecture his entire life. Bought it his entire life as well. Placed the lessons before everything else.

He let his mind drift back to a few moments earlier and the way Roxy's face had shimmered oh-so-temptingly under the fluorescent light. What would dear old Dad say about reputation if he knew his namesake was fantasizing about a client?

Not wanting to lose the fantasy, he clicked off the phone, figuring he could always blame a dropped call. He really wasn't in the mood to listen to his father's reminders about family obligations right now. They could come back to haunt him another time.

Right now he wanted to think about his client.

CHAPTER EIGHT

"WILL you stop fidgeting?" Mike reached over and took the fork from Roxanne's hand before she could tap it against the tablecloth again. "It makes you look nervous."

"I *am* nervous," she shot back.

"Doesn't mean you have to let the whole restaurant know."

They were seated in the dining room of the Landmark. He'd selected the stately hotel because its old-money feel made for a good backdrop. Not to mention, it kept the reporter from seeing how slow work was back at his office.

"Shouldn't you have learned how to pretend in acting school?" he asked her.

"I was a lousy actress, remember?" She'd moved to fiddling with her napkin, smoothing and resmoothing the cloth across her lap.

"I remember." Sadly he also completely understood the nerves. His own stomach was doing the Mexican hat dance. They both had a lot riding on this interview. Done right, and Julie's column would spawn other articles. TV coverage. Enough notoriety the Sinclairs would have to act. Screw up, and the Sinclairs could write her off as another crackpot looking for fifteen minutes of fame.

Lord, but it had to work. Under the table, he felt his own knee start to jiggle. He squeezed his thigh.

"You'll be fine," he told Roxy. Taking a page from his own advice, he refused to let her see his agitation. "Just don't say things like 'I can't believe they charge seventeen dollars for a fruit plate.'"

"But I can't believe it."

"I know." The price didn't exactly sit well with him, either. He was beginning to worry about how much money the case was costing him. Not that he'd say so to Roxy. After all, like everyone else, she saw him as a big, uptown lawyer.

"How much longer before she gets here?" she asked.

Mike checked his watch. She was five minutes late. "Soon. Any minute probably."

"Great." He felt the floor jiggling. It was her knee bouncing now.

"Relax. You remember all the answers we rehearsed, don't you?"

"I do."

"Then you have nothing to worry about."

"And you're sure I look all right?"

"I promise, you look fine." More than fine, actually. To his immense pleasure, her hair was less straight, the curls framing her face while a clasp held the rest at the base of her neck. She wore a pale blue cashmere turtleneck and camel hair slacks, with a brown suede jacket. Around her neck she wore a strand of pearls. Her mother's. A far cry from the woman who'd walked into his office a few weeks earlier.

He couldn't help himself. He had to reach over and give her fingers a reassuring squeeze, regardless of whether Julie walked in. The smile Roxanne beamed at him made the gesture worth it. "Thank you."

Before the moment could go any further he spotted the reporter approaching the dining room. He slipped his hand from Roxy's, trying not to feel the chill the absence of contact brought, and waved her over. "Ready?" he asked, rising.

"Ready as I'll ever be."

Julie greeted him with a kiss on the cheek, then extended her hand. "Roxanne O'Brien? Julie Kinogawa from the *Daily Press*. Mike tells me you've got an interesting story to share."

Mike sat back and watched as Roxy took over and told her story the way they rehearsed it. Plainly and honestly. When she got to the part about Steffi, she didn't flinch, admitting her mistakes with the same brutal frankness she used when telling him. It wasn't easy for her. And it wasn't easy to hear. When Mike saw the telltell brown that signaled her eyes were about to moisten, he felt that overwhelming urge to stop the interview and take her in his arms. He didn't, but dammit, it took a lot of effort. When she finished, he didn't know if Julie bought a word. But he was charmed out of his ever loving mind.

"Oh, my God! I can't believe I got through that without making a complete fool of myself!" They were in the Landmark Lobby, having said goodbye to Julie a few minutes earlier. Roxy wanted to fly, she was so hyped up. The interview couldn't have gone better. Soon as Julie started asking questions, the answers flowed out of her. It was as though she became the part she was supposed to be playing—Roxanne O'Brien, long-lost heiress. Then again, she was Roxanne O'Brien, long-lost heiress, wasn't she? She wanted to giggle, the thought seemed so fantastic.

"I was afraid I'd break down when I started to talk about Steffi, but I kept it together. I think because Julie seemed so understanding. I think she knew why I wanted to keep my daughter out of the spotlight. Is she a mother? Oh, God, listen to me. I'm talking a mile a minute."

Mike laughed. Lord, but she never noticed how lyrical a laugh he had before. Why hadn't she noticed? "It's nice to see you excited," he said.

"Oh, I'm excited all right." Excited like she'd downed a half dozen energy drinks.

Turning to face him, she walked backward, relying on her energy to guide her through the space. "She seemed really interested in what I had to say, don't you think? I mean, like really, really interested." She paused. "Or am I being naive?"

"Well, it wouldn't be the first time a reporter feigned friendliness, then did a hatchet job," Mike said.

Roxy's insides froze. Crap. That would be so like her luck.

"But—" coppery reassurance lit up his eyes "—I don't think this is the case."

"I hope you're right." His approval shouldn't feel so good, but it did. It washed through her like a wave, leaving behind a radiant glow that made her feel like the most special woman alive. "I was afraid I'd screw it up."

"All you had to do was tell the truth. How could you screw that up?"

"You'd be surprised."

"Well, you better get used to telling it. If all goes according to plan, this time next week, you'll be flooded with interview offers from around the city. The Sinclair sisters won't have a choice but to acknowledge your existence."

Acknowledge her existence. Hearing those three words, the magnitude of what was about to happen hit her full-on. For once, luck was breaking her way. Life was breaking her way.

"Oh, my God! This is really happening, isn't it?" With a giddy squeal that was worthy of Steffi, she spun around on her toes. Finally her mother's dying words were going to actually have a legacy besides confusion. She was going to become an heiress! "I can't believe it!"

"I hate to say I told you so, but…"

"You can say it all you want." Far as Roxy was concerned, he was the fairy godmother who made this all come true. "If it weren't for your ad in the directory, none of this would be happening."

Aw, hell. She felt way too magnanimous for simple words. She flung her arms around his neck. "Thank you for everything," she murmured against his shoulder.

His jacket smelled like him, the invitingly masculine scent wrapping around her as surely as his arms. She pressed her cheek to his lapel. Not for long. A second or two. Just long enough for the moment for the aroma to reach inside her. When she pulled back, his arms stayed locked, keeping her trapped in his cocoon. The rest of the world faded away. Looking up, all Roxy could see was the burned copper of his gaze and that perfect shaped mouth.

Who leaned in first didn't matter. Their mouths collided, the kiss desperate and long overdue. Roxy tightened her grip. She couldn't get enough. Couldn't get close enough. Her body was pressed to the length of him, and she still wanted closer—wanted more—with an intensity that she knew would scare the hell out of her once the moment ended.

When the kiss did break, they stood foreheads pressed together, breathless. Roxy wondered if the earth had tipped over. She felt off balance, shaken. She had to clutch Mike's forearms to keep from falling over. "I—I—"

"That—" Mike sounded as shaken as her. His hands were wrapped around her arms; the blood pulsing in his fingertips, discernible through her sweater.

"That was—"

"Definitely a mistake."

Mike's words struck her, hard, recalling the intensity she'd found so frightening a few seconds before. A mistake. He was right.

"Yes," she said, stepping backward. "It was." Right? There was no reason for his words to sound so disheartening.

"I'm your lawyer. You're a client. It's wrong."

"Right. I mean, of course."

"I mean, it's unethical. It's a violation of my legal oath."

She moved farther away, to a railing near the marble steps. Gripping the cold polished brass helped to cool her thoughts if not her insides. "I understand."

But he seemed intent on adding further arguments anyway. "Plus, now you've talked with the press. If Julie or someone else were to see us…"

"I understand. Really, I do." Despite the hollow feeling in the pit of her stomach. "There's Steffi, too. If she were to think we were…you know… then she might get the wrong impression, and I don't want her getting hurt."

The look passing across his face had to be relief. She refused to think it was anything else because that would only put the thought in her head as well. And she didn't want to think anything but relief. "So we agree."

"One hundred percent," Roxy told him. "I let this morning's excitement get me carried away."

"Me, too." He tried a smile. "Guess we chalk it up to gratitude and adrenaline were a dangerous combination."

"Absolutely. It won't happen again."

"No," he agreed. "It won't."

Good, Roxy thought to herself. Better yet, now that the itch was out of her system, maybe she wouldn't be so strangely drawn to every little thing he did or said. Or want to study every expression that crossed his face.

Maybe the longing his presence produced, and that, at the moment, ached stronger than ever, would fade away as well.

CHAPTER NINE

MIKE slapped the lease notice on his desk with a frustrated sigh. It had been two weeks since Julie's column ran in the *Daily Press. Modern Day Anastasia Wants Answers; To Claim Her Role in Sinclair Legacy.* The *Press* believed in over-the-top headlines. Still, the piece worked. Roxy had been asked for interviews from several radio stations, two local affiliates and a national lifestyle magazine. As expected a few unsolicited pieces ran, too. A couple reporters found their way to the Elderion and one poked around Roxy's apartment building writing about her "dubious" roommates. Roxy's candid rebuttal to that piece ran in Julie's column today. Pieces also appeared.

And yet, despite all this media activity, silence from Jim Brassard and the Sinclairs. Even he was beginning to be concerned. Of course, when Roxy asked, he made a point of dodging the answer. He didn't want to upset her while she was meeting with the media.

Or rather upset her more than he already had. Like it had all week, his blood shot straight to his groin as the memory of their kiss came flooding forward. In fact, *kiss* was far too benign a word. All-out assault on his senses? Better.

He told her they should blame the rush of the moment. If that was true, then why was his brain still screaming *More! More! More!*

Way to blur the lines, Templeton. He spun around his chair to stare at the building behind him. Fifteen years ago he made a call. Career and expectations first, personal desires and interests second. It was the only way he'd be able to achieve the level of success his family wanted from him, and thus far, it had served him well. Now was not the time to back off.

He swiveled back around, accidentally scattering Wentworth's letters with his arm. Bending over, he retrieved the trio that fell to the floor. In his final letter, Wentworth had been full of promises and decisions. He was coming home and telling his parents he was leaving Harvard and marrying Fiona, damn the consequences. Wonder what would have happened if Wentworth had made the trip home safely? Would he have carried through with his plans?

The question made him think, with more than a little guilt, about Grace. Fifteen years ago, coward that he was, he took the exact opposite track from Wentworth. Chose the route mapped out for him. That he did so easily told him Grace wasn't as great a passion as he remembered. Backing away from Roxanne yesterday had been harder.

Wonder what he'd do if he had to make the same decision today?

He didn't have time to ponder the thought for long. The phone rang. Soon as the caller identified himself, everything else became unimportant.

"Steffi, please. Hurry up and finish your dinner so we can get to Mrs. Ortega's. I have to get to work." High-heeled toe tapping on the carpeting, Roxy gave her daughter a stern look. Why was it kids were always their slowest when you needed them to move quickly?

At the dining room table, Steffi poked her meat loaf with her fork. "I don't like it," she said.

"You said you liked it when we had it two nights ago."

"Now it's old."

Roxy took a deep breath. She would not lose her patience. No matter if the clock over the stove told her she had about ten minutes to catch her bus.

Truth was, she couldn't completely blame her daughter for being cranky. With all these interviews and meetings, she'd had to spend more and more time at the babysitter's. What was the alternative? Leaving her here to hang with Wayne?

"Can I have more milk?" Steffi asked.

"When you've finished your meat loaf." Nice try, kid, but she was hip to that game; fill up on milk so you were too full to eat. The little girl whined. After giving another quick look at the clock, Roxy squatted so she was at eye level. Her spandex skirt rose distressingly high on her thighs. Since she'd changed up her wardrobe, she found the waitress uniform increasingly uncomfortable. The skirt was too tight and the camisole showed way too much cleavage.

Actually, it was more than the uniform. Simply going to work at the club had become more difficult too. Each day spent meeting with reporters and being treated like she was somebody, made hauling vodka tonics in a pair of high heels worse. It was like she'd finally gotten a tiny glimpse of what the world could possibly become. Except despite the interviews, they still hadn't heard from the Sinclairs. Mike told her not to worry. Then again, he also never answered her questions about the Sinclairs directly anymore, either, preferring to reassure her instead. His way of avoiding having to give her bad news.

Mike. Thinking of the mind-blowing kiss they shared wasn't doing her mood any favors. All it did was create a hot, needy sensation in the pit of her stomach. It stunk that the worst ideas were always the ones that nagged you.

Steffi still wasn't eating her meat loaf. "Baby, if you don't finish your dinner, you and Dusty won't get any dessert."

"Leave the kid alone. I wouldn't eat that warmed-up stuff, either."

"You're not helping, Alexis," Roxy said.

"Just sayin', I'd take her to that fast food burger place."

"Can we, Mommy?"

"No, Steffi."

"But I want chicken nuggets."

"Stephanie Rose O'Brien, finish your meat loaf."

Still swearing to keep her patience, she followed her roommate into the kitchen. Alexis had been as bad as Steffi lately. Worse ever since the *Daily Press* article appeared, though really Roxy thought the article was only part of a bigger issue.

"By the way," she said, "why didn't you tell me the package from AM America arrived?"

"Excuse me," the heavier woman replied, as she grabbed a bag of cheese curls from the pantry. "I didn't know I was your secretary now."

"You're not," Roxy replied. Her patience at treading lightly was wearing thin. "But I told you

I was waiting for it. Would it hurt to say something?"

"Sorry. Must be my susceptible side."

"Disreputable," Roxy said. A correction that earned her an eye roll. "I cleared all that up. Didn't you read Julie's column today?

"You mean your big speech about how people shouldn't judge you because of where you live or who you hang out with?"

"People. I said *people* shouldn't be judged by who they associate with. I was lumping you in with me."

"Gee, thanks. Did your boyfriend suggest you say something like that?"

"Mike isn't my boyfriend." Damn, if she didn't feel an ache clear through to her heart at the mention of his name.

"Whatever."

Oh, for crying out loud. She was getting pretty sick and tired of the comments. Roxy stepped over to the countertop. "What's really bugging you? You've been copping an attitude for two weeks."

"Maybe I don't like being dissed."

"I corrected that in Julie's column."

"Oh, right. You say a few snotty things to your new BFF Julie and that's supposed to make it all better?"

Snotty? It was a correction for crying out loud.

She didn't have to do anything. "So what would make it better then?"

Alexis shrugged. "You tell me. You're the one with all the fancy uptown friends now. Why don't you ask your sugar daddy next time he takes you shopping or to one of your fancy lunches?"

Is that what this was all about? Her new wardrobe? Going out to eat?

"Get over yourself," her roommate replied at the suggestion. "All I'm saying is while you're running around with reporters and going to fancy restaurants, Wayne and I are still back here waiting for ours."

"Maybe if Wayne stopped sitting…" Roxy muttered.

Alexis slammed the cabinet door, making Roxy jump. "I'm getting pretty sick of you trashing my baby brother every time you turn around."

"Then we're even because I'm sick of him living on my couch." She hadn't forgotten the disgusting word he muttered to her the other day. A word his sister had to have heard and said nothing about. "I've told you before I don't like him around Steffi. And you're stupid if you think I don't know what kind of 'business' he's doing in this neighborhood."

"Oh, now you're calling me stupid? Excuse me,

but not everyone's lucky enough to have a mother get knocked up by a millionaire.

"But you know that," she added, her mouth full of orange cheese.

Roxy squeezed her fists. "You leave Steffi out of this."

"I wasn't talking about Steffi. I was talking about you, acting like you're all better than us. And don't forget," she said, slicing the air with an orange index finger, "I pay half the rent here. You don't want your kid around my brother, then go live with your boyfriend."

"He's not my—" Roxy didn't have time to argue. She'd deal with this after work. Provided she still had a job. Dion was ticked off at her about reporters, too. "Come on, Steffi. Go get your coat."

"But you said I could have dessert."

"You'll have to have dessert at Mrs. Ortega's. Mommy's really late."

"I don't want to go to Mrs. Ortega's. You promised. I want ice cream!" The four-year-old began to cry, the loud, unreasonable gulps of a tantrum.

Naturally. Roxy lifted the little girl from her chair, wincing as her squirming legs banged her exposed thighs. The pain hurt less than the guilt.

"You promised!" Steffi chanted over and over. She might as well have been saying "You're the worst mother in the world. I hate you", and even though she knew the world wouldn't end because of one missed dessert, Roxy couldn't help feeling like her daughter was right.

Adding insult to injury, as the door shut behind her and a still crying Steffi, she could hear Wayne and Alexis laughing.

"Well, look who decided to grace us with her presence," Jackie drawled when she finally managed to rush in, twenty minutes late.

So not what she needed right now. "Sorry I'm late, Dion," she said, tying on her apron. "Steffi gave me a hard time about going to the sitter's."

"So glad you could fit us in your schedule," he replied. "I gave Jackie your tables one through four."

"What?" He was cutting down her groups? "Why?"

"Because I needed someone to cover them, and she showed up on time."

Great. Just great. First Steffi, then Alexis, now she'd have to make do with half her tip money. Was the whole world conspiring against her tonight?

"Not like you need the money anyway, seeing how you're an heiress now."

"I'm not an heiress yet." Soon as she said it,

Roxy realized how off-putting the comment sounded.

"Reminds me," Dion said. "I caught another one of those reporters poking around, asking the customers questions."

"I'm sorry." The articles that appeared earlier in the week ticked him off. "Least it's free publicity."

"Oh, yeah, the owner's thrilled with the place being called shabby."

"Maybe he'll spring for an upgrade." The place certainly needed it.

The bartender didn't appreciate the suggestion. "Maybe you should get your butt in gear and wait on customers before I give Jackie more of your tables."

Without another word, Roxy grabbed her pad and tray, making sure she moved quick enough that neither Dion nor Jackie saw her eyes getting wet. Why was the whole world so angry with her? She didn't ask for her mother to have an affair with Wentworth Sinclair. Why were they all out to punish her now?

If Mike were here, he'd understand.

Soon as the thought formed in her brain, she froze in her tracks. What the heck? A few weeks ago, her insides ran screaming at the idea of leaning on anyone, let alone him. Now here she was desperate to cry on his shoulder. What the heck happened to her?

Mike happened, that's what. Mike and his coppery, reassuring gaze and his day at the park.

This, she thought, was why kissing him had been a bad idea. Why she agreed with him it couldn't happen again, despite being the most mind-blowing kiss she'd ever had. She was getting too attached, too reliant on the man. Seeing him as more than a lawyer. A useless point since the other day, while standing in the Landmark, he made it quite clear that his being a lawyer came first.

Her first table ordered bottled beer. Same with the second. Dion not only reassigned her tables, but he left her with the ones who weren't going to spend any money. The night was getting better and better. Only one thing would make this disaster complete and that was…

"Hello, Roxy."

Mike was sitting at table eight. Karma really felt like kicking her in the butt today, didn't it?

Definitely. Why else would he look absolutely spectacular, in a beige suit she'd never seen before and a striped shirt? Shadows danced across his cheekbones, creating hollows and highlighting planes. Roxy's insides melted upon sight. Knowing her reaction wasn't merely physical was making it worse. She'd felt her spirits lift as soon as she heard his voice.

Suddenly she realized the problem with Mike wasn't a matter of becoming too attached; she *was* attached. Very, very attached. Oh, man, but she was in trouble, wasn't she?

She tucked nonexistent hair behind her ears. "Fancy meeting you here. Got tired of your office?"

"What can I say? There's something about this place that keeps drawing me back." He smiled, and the rest of the club receded. "You got a minute?"

"Not right now. Dion's upset because I was late. Problem with Steffi."

"Nothing serious, I hope."

Seeing his expression change and become serious did nothing to stop the emotion weaving its way through her. In fact, her heart grew. "No. She's tired of going to the babysitter is all."

"Well, Mrs. Ortega does smell like arthritis rub."

"True." *And you smell like wool and Dial soap and have arms that make a woman feel secure and safe.*

She had to shake these thoughts from her head. They weren't doing either of them any good. "Can you stick around till my break?"

"Of course."

"I'll get you the usual then."

Making her way to the bar, she tried to decide if his sticking around was good or not. For the past couple weeks, since the kiss, they'd managed to keep their dealings businesslike and short, involving a third party as often as possible. But tonight, with her working the crowd and wearing this skimpy outfit, knowing his eyes were going to be on her... Maybe risking Dion's anger was the better decision after all.

She purposely waited until she'd served all her other tables before bringing him his drink. She wasn't sure why, except that having an empty tray made it less likely she'd become distracted and ignore her customers. Make that more distracted. His looming presence would be permanently stuck in the front of her brain from now until her break.

It took like what seemed most of the night, but Dion finally gave her a break. "We'll have to be quick," she told Mike, slipping into the chair across from him. "Dion made it very clear I couldn't take a second more than ten minutes." *He wants more, he can meet you at his office,* the bartender had snarked.

"Still angry about the articles, huh."

"Everybody's mad," Roxy replied. "Alexis and Wayne are mad, Steffi's mad, Jackie and Dion are mad. They all think I've gone uptown and think I'm too good for them."

"They're right."

Mike's answer surprised her. Wasn't this the same man who insisted on a makeover? "You sure you didn't have a few pops before you got here?" she asked.

"Not a drop. You're better than all this, Roxanne. If the rest of the world can't see that, then the world's full of idiots."

The moisture returned to her eyes forcing her to blink. Dammit. How was she supposed to unattach herself if he was going to behave so nicely?

Along with reaching across the table to brush a tear from her cheek the way he was doing now. His touch was soft and sweet. She had to fight not to lean into his palm. "Thank you for the pep talk," she said, managing a bit of a smile.

"You're welcome. I have something else that might cheer you up more."

"Really?" She started to ask when she saw his grin. Only one thing would make him smile that wide and look that confident. Her heart stopped beating. "Don't tell me..."

"Jim Brassard called me earlier this evening."

"Are you saying...?"

His wide grin grew wider. "The Sinclair sisters want to meet you."

CHAPTER TEN

IN NEW YORK society circles, Alice and Frances Sinclair were considered eccentric icons. Both twice divorced, they lived together in the Gramercy Park brownstone where they grew up while their children lived in more modern penthouses nearby. Between the two of them, the Sinclair name was part of almost every charitable board in the city.

Roxy's knees shook as they stood in front of the iron gate. "What if they don't like me?" she whispered in Mike's ear.

"You asked the same thing about Julie. Be yourself and everything will be fine."

Roxy wished she shared his confidence, but she couldn't shake the feeling of anxiety crawling along the back of her neck. For all she knew, the Sinclairs wanted to see her so they could tell her to her face to buzz off.

"Remember, you're their family." As usual Mike seemed to read her thoughts and say the words she needed to hear. What would she do when she didn't have him standing by her side anymore?

She couldn't bear to think about it.

A metallic-sounding voice came on the gate speaker to greet them. Mike introduced themselves and a moment later, the gate clicked open.

"Promising sign."

"Unless there are dogs about to run at us."

"That's my girl. Mistrustful as ever."

Because she'd never been this close to good fortune before. Sixty minutes from now she could be...

Dear God, she was too afraid to form the words.

The ornately carved main entrance sat back from the curb, a short cement walkway protecting the sisters from the noise of the street. No more than six feet, it felt like six hundred. Two steps in, Roxy felt a reassuring pressure at the curve of her elbow. "Making sure you don't trip in those shoes," he said in a soft voice.

"I'm wearing flats."

"You still never know." He gave her elbow a squeeze, sending waves of reassurance up her arm. Roxy felt so cherished in that one moment, she swore her heart grew too big for her heart. *Oh, how she loved this man.*

Before she could argue with herself about her choice of words, they reached the front door and a suited servant opened it. A middle-age woman in a crisp black suit came walking up just behind. "I'm Millicent Webster, the sisters' secretary," she greeted, in a polite and formal voice. "They're waiting for you in the solarium. If you follow me, I'll take you."

Roxy wasn't sure what a solarium was, but she quickly surmised it was another name for sunroom as they were led down a corridor to a large, window-filled room in the rear of the house. When they arrived, they found the two elderly women seated side by side in matching Queen Anne chairs. They were chatting with a gray-haired man sitting on the sofa. The man immediately stood up. "Good afternoon, Mike. Thank you for coming." He looked straight at Roxy. "And you must be Roxanne O'Brien."

Roxy cleared her throat. "Yes," she whispered. Over in their chairs, the Sinclair sisters were staring intently; she could feel the scrutiny.

The gasp when she walked in didn't help, either.

"I'm Jim Brassard, the Sinclair family attorney. May I introduce Frances and Alice Sinclair."

Frances, the taller of the two motioned for them to take a seat. "We're so glad you could meet with us. Aren't we, Alice?"

"Yes, we are." Alice was a few inches smaller, with bright black eyes that matched her sister's.

Both had short-cropped hair and strong features. For the first time Roxy noticed the giant New-foundland sprawled between the chairs. She just knew there would be dogs. Though this one didn't look too threatening.

"This is Bunty," Frances said, following her line of sight. "He's been with us forever. My second husband bought him as a puppy. Turns out he was the only thing worth salvaging about the relation-ship. Don't worry. He won't bite. Poor creature hasn't moved fast in years."

Mike chuckled. Roxy managed a wan smile. Her pulse was racing, making breathing, let alone making noise, difficult. Smoothing the front of her slacks, she perched on the edge of the sofa, where Frances had indicated.

"Thank you for being willing to talk with us," she heard Mike say. "I know this must be awk-ward for you."

"Our family, by nature, is very private," Frances replied. "We aren't one to seek publicity." She cocked her head. "But you already knew that, didn't you, Mr. Templeton."

Roxy looked up in time to see his cheeks blush a sheepish tinge. "I might have heard something to that effect. We weren't trying to embarrass the family, I assure you. Simply get your attention."

"Well, you did. Get our attention," Jim said.

Meanwhile, Alice was still studying her. The probing made Roxy want to squirm her way behind the sofa cushions. Nervously she tucked her hair behind her ear.

"Alice, stop," Frances snapped, realizing. "You're making the girl uncomfortable."

"I'm sorry. I don't mean to. It's just…that hair and your eyes. I knew as soon as I saw your photograph in the newspaper."

"Knew?" Roxy asked.

"How much you resemble your mother."

They knew her mother. Roxy couldn't believe it.

"We didn't know her name," Frances continued. "Both Alice and I were married and living elsewhere at the time. But she worked for us. As a weekend maid."

"It was the hair," Alice said. "You couldn't forget the hair. Long, strawberry curls. I was so jealous. She had an accent, too, I believe."

"Irish," Roxy supplied. "She came from County Cork as a little girl. I'm confused, though. Are you sure it was my mother? I thought she worked for a hotel."

"She might have. Father let the whole staff go one summer. At the time, we wondered what set him off."

"Then again something was always setting father off," Frances said. "He had a very short temper."

"Finding out his son was involved with one of the staff could certainly anger a man," Mike said.

"I certainly remember how upset Wenty was when he found out. I had stopped by and he was pacing back and forth fuming. Told me he didn't want to talk about it. It was a couple weeks before he left for Cambridge, I believe."

"We didn't talk to him nearly enough that semester," Frances said softly.

"No, we didn't."

Sisterly regret hung in the air. No matter what happened regarding her, she suspected Alice and Frances loved their baby brother, and wanted to do right for him. She looked to her lap, trying to imagine how events unfolded. Her mother, fresh out of high school, coming to work for the Sinclairs, meeting a young Wentworth. The two of them growing closer, then intimate. Powell Sinclair finding out and firing the entire staff.

"You never saw her again after that?" Mike asked.

"Why would we? Shortly after, Wenty left for Cambridge. He was at Harvard. We were both trying to build marriages."

"Fat lot that did," Alice muttered.

And the redhead was nothing more than a former, fired staff member. No reason to follow up. Why indeed? Her mother's failure to talk with the Sinclairs was starting to make sense now. She must have feared what Powell would do.

"Then before we knew it, Wenty died. He should never have been driving so fast."

"He was eager to get home," Jim Brassard said.

"He was rushing home for a reason," Mike told him. He reached into his back pocket and dropped the stack of letters in Roxy's lap. Still looking down, Roxy ran her finger over the velvet ribbon. Mike had told her what Wentworth's final few letters said. His final promises to the woman he loved. She'd given the press a brief overview of the stack's content, but only the broadest of strokes. These pages were the couple's final intimate moments.

"My mother held on to these for thirty years," she told the sisters, holding out the stack.

"Wentworth's final letters," Frances declared. "You mentioned them in your interviews."

The older woman withdrew the top letter. "May we?"

"Please."

Time ticked off on a nearby floor clock. Roxy and Mike waited while the sisters and Jim Brassard read the letters in silence. At some point, a staff member brought in a tea service. Watching the woman set down the tray, Roxy wondered what her mother would think, her sitting as a guest in the solarium thirty years after she got tossed out. Was this what she wanted? *I hope so, Mom.*

She stole a glance to her left. Mike looked right at home. His suit, his bearing—they fit in. No surprise. What did surprise her was how comfortable she felt. This was her father's home. Her family's home. The notion made her smile. Over the rim of his teacup, Mike gave her a wink. Her heart thumped a little harder. Once again, a familiar four-letter word filled her heart. A troublesome four-letter word if true. Love wasn't on the agenda. Not with a man who considered kissing her a mistake.

Examining her feelings for her lawyer, though, would have to wait. Having read enough, the sisters set the letters down and offered a pair of polite coughs.

"Wentworth was always dramatic," Alice remarked. "Whatever his interest, he threw himself in with a passion for as long as he was involved."

"I think his relationship with Roxanne's mother was more than a casual interest," Mike said.

"Oh, I have no doubt they were in love and that he intended to issue an ultimatum to our father," Frances said.

"He was always issuing ultimatums," Alice

added. "It was part of his passionate nature. Once, when he discovered our father was investing in a Japanese venture, he went on a hunger strike. Said he wouldn't eat until he had proof the company wasn't involved in harming dolphins."

Her older sister nodded and reverently slid the letter back into the envelope. "That was one of his more over-the-top demonstrations."

Roxy listened to them in disbelief. They weren't seriously equating his love affair with her mother with dolphin-safe fishing? "Forgive me, but those letters—"

"Oh, I know," Alice cut her off. "They are amazingly detailed."

"To say the least," Jim Brassard muttered. "You weren't kidding, Mike."

"And, I have no doubt that he believed every word at the time," Frances said. "Whether he was serious about his threats is something we'll never know."

"He gave up the hunger strike after thirty-six hours," Alice said in a soft voice.

"Still." Frances squared her shoulders. "Fact remains that when he wrote these letters, he was in love, and I think, given your story, your mother loved him. If there were consequences to their love affair, it's our responsibility to see to them."

"Are you saying what I think you're saying?" Mike asked.

Roxy held her breath for the answer. If she heard right, Frances and Alice were willing to… No, she wouldn't believe until she heard the words straight from one of the sister's mouths.

"The Sinclairs place a high value on responsibility and on family. If our brother fathered a child, then that child is part of our family. We won't turn our backs on her existence."

Oh, my goodness, she was saying what Roxy thought she said.

"The question is," the woman continued, showing marks of the shrewdness that made her father a scion of business. "What are your motives, Miss O'Brien?"

"I want the truth." Roxy had been thinking about this for a while now. "More than anything, I want to know the truth. I want to know who I am."

Both women smiled and gave slight nods of their heads. Her answer apparently pleased them. "That's what we'd like as well," Frances replied. "We'll be glad to cooperate with your DNA test, Miss O'Brien."

Pop! Champagne foamed up and down the side of the bottle. Roxy laughed as Mike held it up to keep it from running onto his desk. "Not my neatest opening," he said. "But what's the point of splurging on champagne if you can't be messy?"

"Good point."

They picked up the bottle on the way back from Gramercy Park, feeling the need to cap off the meeting with a celebration. Tomorrow they would go to a local lab so Roxy could have her cheek swabbed for DNA. If lucky, they'd have the results within a week.

Best part of everything had been the sisters themselves. After they agreed to the test, the pair shared with her the family photo albums. She saw pictures of Wentworth as a child and as he looked a few months before he died. Call her crazy, but she could see a little of Steffi in his face. Around the jaw and the chin.

She watched Mike pour champagne into the two ceramic mugs on his desk. "Pretty big drinks," she said, noting they were three-quarters full.

"Big celebrations call for big drinks," he replied, handing her one. "Why, you got somewhere to be?"

Actually she did. Work. "I'm supposed to be at the Lounge in—" She looked at her watch. Shoot! Was it really that late? "I was supposed to be at work fifteen minutes ago."

In a flash, Mike set down his cup, and was on his feet. "I'll drive you."

"It's okay."

"You sure?"

"There's no need." She'd only be rushing to a job that no longer existed. Dion made it very clear at the end of last night's shift, he wouldn't tolerate any more missed time. "I'm pretty sure I'm now unemployed."

"I'm sorry."

"Yeah, me, too." Surprised her how casual she sounded. You'd think she'd be more upset about becoming unemployed. She simply couldn't work up the angst right now.

"What about Steffi? Do we need to get her?"

"She's at Mrs. Ortega's till midnight, and given Alexis's mood lately, it's the best place for her. The less time we're in the apartment, the better."

"Still giving you a hard time, hey?"

"Worse this morning than last night. I didn't dare tell her about our meeting."

She sighed. When Alexis first moved in, the relationship seemed like it had such potential. "I can't wait to get Steffi out of that environment."

"If things go well, you'll be able to move anywhere you'd like," he said, handing her a cup. "To positive DNA tests."

Roxy clinked her mug against his. "To scaling Mt. Everest barefoot. And having a kick-ass attorney."

She took a sip and grimaced at the dry flavor. Guess it was an acquired taste.

Mike set down his drink.

"I wouldn't start patting ourselves on the back too soon. We passed a big hurdle getting them to agree to the DNA test, but we haven't scaled the peak yet. After the results are in, we still have to prove you deserve a share of the estate. I know the sisters said they wanted to do right by their brother's family, but Jim Brassard is going to do whatever he can to protect their assets. He can make it a hell of a fight if he wants to."

"But I've got you." Roxy wasn't worried. She had faith Mike would succeed. He'd gotten her this far, hadn't he?"

Imagine that. Roxy O'Brien having faith. Who'd have thought that a month ago. She took another drink, this time finding the champagne a little more appealing.

"What?" she asked, catching him watching. There was so much tender curiosity in his eyes. Shivers danced along her skin, matching the bubbles in her cup.

"You look very pensive all of a sudden," he said.

"I was thinking how much things can change in a month. Four weeks ago I stormed out of this office thinking you were a condescending, arrogant jerk."

"And now?"

Now I can't imagine a day without you in it. "Now I'm sitting here drinking champagne." To punctuate her point, she took a sip. "I'm glad I left one of my letters behind."

"Me, too."

Coming around to her side of the desk, he sat down next to her. His hip brushed against hers causing the air between them to crackle. Roxy thought about shifting, but the contact felt too nice. She liked the warmth spreading though her body.

"I have a confession to make," he said.

"What's that?"

"I would have tracked you down anyway. I wanted the case."

For the moment, Roxy pretended he didn't say the second line, and focused on him tracking her down. "Well, if this is going to be honesty time, I suppose I owe you an apology."

"You mean for something other than thinking I was arrogant and condescending?"

"Yes," she replied, bumping his shoulder. Wow, had she really already drank half her cup? The stuff grew on you. "When you said you would win this case, you told me you never said anything you couldn't back up. I didn't believe you."

"You might want to hold off on that. Like I said, we haven't won yet."

"But I was wrong to doubt you, your abilities." She stared at the bubbles rising from the golden liquid and popping, creating tiny little sprays in her mug. "Your sincerity. Your confidence. I shouldn't have.

"To Mike Templeton," she said, raising her glass. "The winner he said he was."

"Don't."

What'd she say? He stood up, taking his warmth and his contact with him as he headed to the picture window. The air grew cold. "I thought you wanted me to believe in you."

"Believe your case had a chance, yes. But—" He looked out to some place far away. "I'm not a winner, Roxy."

"Don't be silly." Of course he was. He'd been a winner his whole life. He told her so. "We won today, didn't we?"

He opened his mouth to protest, but she waved it off. He could talk about waiting until the case was over and all that, but as far as she was concerned, he had won today. He'd won her faith.

And maybe a little more? Maybe her heart?

She slipped off the desk, surprised when the floor swayed a little. Stupid floor.

For the third time today, she wondered if her feelings ran deeper than simple gratitude. "Third time's a charm, isn't it?" a voice in her head asked.

Possibly. Romance so wasn't on her agenda. He was the wrong man, the wrong person to fall for. And yet, here she was.

She joined him at the window. Between the night outside, and the fluorescent office lights, his face was cast in shadows. He looked sad. Regretful. Slipping in front of him, she sat on the window heater. "What's with the modesty all of a sudden?"

"Speaking the truth is all," he replied. "I don't like to take credit for something that isn't my accomplishment."

"Whose accomplishment is it?"

He blinked, and looked at her with surprise. "Yours, of course. If you win, if you prove you're a Sinclair and get your share of the inheritance, you'll be the reason why."

"Well, sure." She took another long drink. Silly man. "It's my DNA. Still, I couldn't have done anything without you. Don't sell yourself short, Counselor." She giggled the last word because the bubbles chose that moment to tickle her nose.

"I am a good lawyer, aren't I?"

He said it like discovering a new fact. "Okay," he said, "how about we agree we did this together. To us."

She watched as he tipped back his drink. "We

make a good team, Roxanne O'Brien," he said, topping off his mug.

At the word team, Roxy's heart did a little dance. "You shouldn't say stuff like that unless you mean it," she told him.

"What makes you think I don't?"

Because if she believed him, she'd fall completely under his spell, that's why. As it was, she'd already dropped three-quarters of the way, maybe more.

God, but she felt so good being here with him.

He was topping off her mug again. She didn't mind. The mellow, happy feeling in her limbs felt amazing. She wanted the whole world to feel the same way. The man standing next to her most of all.

"Do you ever loosen your tie?" she asked, swaying toward him.

He laughed. Such an attractive laugh, thought Roxy, taking another drink. Her cup was emptying way too fast, and her head suddenly felt very heavy. So heavy she had to rest her forehead on his chest. Mike's fingers threaded through her hair.

"That's better," she murmured.

"You've had too much champagne," he said. The unnatural lilt in his voice made her giggle.

"S'your fault. Told you the cup was filled too

high." She tried looking up and the room shifted. "I probably should have had something to eat."

"Probably," he replied with a broad smile. With one hand still cradling the back of her head, he used his other to lift his mug and take a long drink. "Same here."

Wow, but he smiled pretty. Could men's smiles be pretty? Never mind, his was. "You haven't answered my question. Do you ever loosen your tie?"

"Haven't since college," he said, giving another one of those adorable laughs. "Got to dress like a Templeton, you know. Can't be seen looking like a bum. Might reflect badly on the family name." Another sip and he leaned in close. "Want to know a secret?"

"Sure." He could tell her anything in that sexy whisper. "What?"

"Sometimes I take my tie off at the end of the day."

"What do you do with it?"

"Depends." He grinned, his eyes shiny like two copper pennies. "On whether or not I've got company."

Oh, my. Roxy's insides turned hot and needy. "It's the end of the day now," she whispered. "And I'm company."

"So you are."

She touched the Windsor knot at his neck. Mike

was right about the alcohol. Her fingers felt thick and clumsy as she undid the silk. Every fumble had her brushing the underside of his chin and caressing his throat. Finally she tugged the cloth loose. "There," she said with a smile. "You're loosened."

"Better?"

"Much." Her smile turned serious as another question came to mind. "Do you really regret kissing me the other day?"

"I never said I regretted it."

"Yes, you did."

"No. I said kissing you was a *mistake*."

"Isn't that the same thing?" Suddenly it was incredibly important for her to know the truth.

"No. A mistake says I shouldn't have done it. Regret implies I was sorry, and I'm not sorry in the least."

Awareness pulsed deep inside her, a low, throbbing need to feel his touch again. Slowly she let her fingers slide from the knot in his tie to the plains of his chest. His hard, chiseled chest. When she reached his heart, her palm flattened and she could feel his heartbeat reaching her through the cloth. The need intensified knowing the rapid beat was because of her. "Would it be a mistake to kiss me again?" she asked, searching his face.

Black eyes, their pupils blown so wide from

desire, searched back. Their heat bore into her. "Yes," he whispered.

Yet he didn't move. "Because I'm your client?"

"No. Because you're tipsy." He cradled her face, his thumbs fanning warm arcs across her cheek. "A gentleman doesn't take advantage of a woman who's been drinking."

He smoothed her eyebrows. "No matter how beautiful and tempting she is."

Roxy leaned closer. "What if I kissed you? Would that be a mistake, too?"

A thrill passed through her seeing his Adam's apple bob hard in his throat. He nodded. "Yes."

"Would you regret it?"

"Question is, would you?"

"Guess we'll have to see, won't we?" Pulling herself on her tiptoes, she pressed her lips to his. The kiss was softer, slower than last time. Roxy's eyes fluttered closed. She concentrated on the feel of Mike's mouth on hers, his taste, the texture of his lips as they massaged hers. She was right; his mouth was perfect. She heard a soft moan escape his throat, and felt his hand cup the back of her skull. Fingers tangled in her hair, angling her face upward. Her lips parted, and for a moment, the kiss became more intimate, a dance of tongues.

The soft caress of his breath on his cheek signaled the dance's end.

"Do you regret that?" she asked, coming down to earth.

He shook his head. "Not one second."

"Good. Because neither do I." If anything, tonight felt right. So very, very right. "What would you do then, if I kissed you a second time?"

"Oh, now, that could be a problem."

"Why?"

Lips, soft and eager, nibbled her jawline. "Because I can't guarantee I'll be able to stop at a simple kiss." To prove his point, he slid his hands down to her bottom and pulled her close so she could feel his arousal.

Smiling, Roxy hooked one leg around his calves and merged their bodies even closer. "Who says I want you to?"

CHAPTER ELEVEN

"FOR goodness' sake, Michael, you really need to check your voice mail. This is my third message in three days. What on earth are you thinking running around doing press interviews with that woman? You are a lawyer, not a—"

Mike switched off the phone midmessage. The woman buttoning her slacks was far more interesting. "Those looked better on the floor," he said with a lazy smile.

Roxanne smiled back. "Wouldn't that make a pretty headline. *Heiress Caught Commuting with Her Pants Down.*"

"I don't know about a headline, but it would definitely make a pretty sight." He ran his hand along the inner thigh he now had intimate knowledge of until she slapped it away.

"Listen to you. The guy who thought my work skirt was too short."

"It was. Doesn't mean I didn't like what I saw."

He frowned. "Why are you talking like you're taking the bus?"

"Well, Mr. Half a Bottle of Champagne, I don't think you're capable of driving, do you?"

"Stay here, then." He pulled her into a deep kiss, grinning when her arms found their way around his neck. "I love how you smell," he murmured, burying his face in the crook of her neck. "I could smell you all night. And taste, and…" He kissed the hollow below her collarbone and was rewarded with a whimper.

Maybe they should take the bus, find an empty backseat….

"I have to go," she said when he finally let her up for air. "I told Mrs. Ortega I'd pick up Steffi at midnight."

"Blast Mrs. Ortega." Much as he wanted to argue the point, he knew she was right. They couldn't leave Steffi at the sitter's indefinitely. Eventually this little celebratory rendezvous would have to end. "Let me put on my shirt and I'll get us a cab."

"Us?" She pulled back. "You know you can't stay, right? I can't have Steffi waking up and getting the wrong impression."

He could argue that, given the environment Roxy and her daughter lived in, his sleeping over was the least detrimental, but he wouldn't. He respected Roxy's protectiveness.

However, she never said he couldn't see her first thing in the morning.

"Breakfast?" she said when he told her.

"When I come get you for the DNA test. I'll bring muffins. Then, after the test is over, if Steffi's still at preschool and there's time..." He ran an index finger down the front of her shirt and hooked the waistband of her pants.

"I'll keep my fingers crossed the lab's running on time," Roxy said.

Catching the mischievous glint in her eyes, Mike couldn't help himself. He kissed her again. Deep and hard. "Down, Counselor," Roxy teased. "Save it for tomorrow.

"By the way," she added, tossing him his shirt, "make sure you bring extra muffins."

"For what?" *Please don't say Wayne and Alexis.*

To his immense pleasure, she didn't. She did, however, give him a quick peck on the cheek. "To keep up your strength, of course."

She slipped out of his arms.

Was he wrong? Mike asked himself while waiting by his reception desk for Roxy to return from the washroom. In the back of his mind, he knew he was supposed to feel guilty. She was a client for crying out loud. How many times over the past few weeks had he reminded himself of the ethical and professional repercussions or lectured himself he had a job to do and that his personal desires meant nothing. Because they'd never mattered before.

Except for tonight. Tonight he'd wanted and he'd taken—for three hours he'd taken—and damn if he wasn't glad. For the first time in a very long time, Mike felt one hundred percent alive.

Was this how Wentworth felt when he was with Fiona? No wonder the guy was planning to fight.

"Ready?

Roxanne stood at the lobby door, her hair still wild from their lovemaking. "Sorry to keep you waiting," she said.

Looking at her, Mike's heart hitched. Amazing how easily tides could turn. A little over a month ago he sat on the edge of failure and judging Roxanne for being rough around the edges. Four and a half weeks later, she was on the cusp of becoming Manhattan's latest socialite and his future was set.

No wonder he felt alive.

He moved toward her, slipping an arm around her waist to lead her toward the door. "No need to apologize," he told her. "You were worth the wait."

"What's a lab tree?" From her perch on top of the counter, Steffi drank her juice from a plastic cup while Roxy moved around the kitchen looking for her coffee mug.

"Laboratory," she corrected. Where was the darn thing? She'd had it a minute ago. "It's a place where people go to get their blood tested."

"Are you sick?"

"Oh, no, baby, I'm not sick." She'd never felt better. To remind herself, she stretched her arms over her head, reveling in the burn of sore muscles from the night before. A soft sigh escaped her lips.

This was the train of thought that caused her to misplace her coffee in the first place.

"Your mama's taking a test to prove she's better than the rest of us." Alexis ambled in, still wearing her nightshirt, and took two mugs from the cabinet.

"Are you better than me?" Steffi asked.

"No one's better than anybody," Roxy replied. "Alexis is making a joke."

From behind the refrigerator door, her roommate coughed. Roxy ignored her. No one was going to ruin her mood, not Alexis. Not even Wayne. In a short while, Mike would be here. Together they'd drop Steffi off at the preschool, go to the lab for her DNA test, and hopefully, if there was time, come back to repeat last night.

For the first time in her life, things were perfect. And, in a few days, when the test results returned, life would become better! She and Steffi would have a full-fledged family tree and the money to build a brand-new life.

She found her coffee. On the dining room table. Cold, but Roxy drank it anyway. Or rather she started to. The phone stopped her.

"Mommy, your phone's ringing." Steffi pointed to the cell on the counter.

Alexis, who'd been standing right next to the phone, looked down and shrugged. "I wouldn't want to mess up one of your interviews," she sneered.

"Never mind, I've got it." Resisting the temptation to get in a snark contest, Roxy simply crossed the room and picked it up. The caller ID said Unknown, but the area code looked familiar.

"Hello?"

"Christina said you're trying to reach me. Said it was important."

Her father. Her other father, that is. Talk about timing. "Yeah, Dad, I wanted to talk to you. It's about Mom."

"There a problem? I thought she had insurance to bury her."

"She did. This is about something else." Taking a deep breath, she asked the multimillion-dollar question. "Did you ever hear of a man named Wentworth Sinclair?"

* * *

Mike drove straight to Roxanne's apartment from his. He'd be early but who cared? Early meant a few extra minutes to say hello. The thought made his body wake up better than any alarm clock.

Fortune continued to smile on him as he snagged a parking spot right in front of the building and stepped onto the sidewalk the same time an elderly man exited the building.

"Someone's getting breakfast delivered," the man said as he held open the front door. He nodded at the wax pastry bag and tray of coffee.

"You can say that again." Mike grinned.

To his surprise, it took three rounds of knocking for Roxanne to open the door. He'd have thought she'd be awake by now, this lab appointment being the apex of everything she wanted. Then again, she did earn the right to be a little tired after last night.

His fist was about to start round four when he finally heard the scrape and jingle of security locks. A second later, Roxanne's face appeared in the doorway. And Mike's insides froze.

One look at the pale skin, the colorless lips, the puffy red eyes, told him she'd been crying. "What's wrong?" he asked, dropping the coffee and muffins on the table. "Is it Steffi?"

"Steffi's fine." She wiped at her cheeks. "My father called."

"Oh, I'm so sorry." He didn't know what else to say. Her distress made sense now. "I wish I'd been here earlier. He didn't take the news well."

"Actually he took the news fine," she said with a sniff. "In fact he knew all about Wentworth and my mom."

What? He did? "And he never said anything after all this time?"

Roxy shook her head. "Didn't see the point. He also told me not to bother taking the test. Because there's absolutely no way I can be Wentworth's daughter."

CHAPTER TWELVE

HE DIDN'T believe her.

"What are you talking about?" he asked, his face the picture of confusion. "Of course you're Wentworth's daughter. The sisters said as much."

"The sisters were wrong. Wentworth died before my mother got pregnant."

"How can you be so certain?"

"Because—" Over on the couch, Steffi sat watching her pony show. Oblivious to the drama playing out around her. Wanting to keep her world undisturbed, Roxy led Mike to the kitchen, where they could talk out of earshot. Her cell phone lay on the counter where she'd dropped it. Right next to the burn mark on the Formica where Wayne left a hot sauce pan and a half-finished cup of coffee. This was her reality. She should have known.

"My father explained everything." Succumbing to the unbearable heaviness that gripped her body, she slumped against the counter. Every last lousy word of their conversation had been cemented in her memory. *You ain't no Sinclair. That was just your mother's wishful thinking.* "Turns out I was born early. The real due date was too far out for me to be Wentworth's."

"Due dates can be fudged."

"Incompetent cervixes can't. Apparently the doctor warned my mother she could go early if she didn't stay off her feet, and she kept working anyway." Why she ignored the doctor's advice, her father didn't say. Maybe they'd been pressed for money or she wanted out of the house.

Or maybe she'd wanted to go early so she could pretend. Keep the fantasy going. "Who knows what went on in that head of hers," her father had said. "She never was all there."

Hearing him speak so bluntly about something so important hurt almost as much as the story itself. Apparently, according to her father, he and her mother met in a local bar, about three weeks after Wentworth's accident. Her mother had been upset. Drinking. He bought her a drink to calm her nerves, and then a second. Next thing they were getting it on in the backseat of his Dodge Dart.

"That's exactly how my father put it, too. Getting it on." She gave a mirthless bark. "Me and my mom, two peas in a pod. Only difference is my dad lived in the same neighborhood, so when my mom found out she was knocked up, she gave him a call. Good Irish Catholic boy that he was, my dad married her."

So much for being the child of some great, unfinished love affair. She was exactly who she always thought she was. A big, unwelcome, unwanted mistake. "My father hadn't left because Fiona still loved Wentworth. He left because he didn't love us enough to stick around."

Roxy dropped her head. All her big plans, her hopes for the future. Killed by a fifteen-minute phone call and a "Sorry, kiddo, I thought you knew."

What a joke. Her gullibility made her sick to her stomach.

Mike was pacing the length of the kitchen. She watched his shoes, thinking how out of place they looked against the scuffed beige flooring. Another reminder of reality. "This can't be happening," he was saying. His muttered words mirrored the voice in her head. "Everything was so damn certain yesterday. What the hell happened?"

"Reality happened," she murmured in reply.

A wash of his hand over his features, his voice steeled. "No need to panic. Not yet. Your father could still have his dates wrong."

If only. "He doesn't."

He stopped his pacing. "You don't know that."

"I know my luck." Why should her paternity

be any different from the other bad choices and failures in her life? What on earth made her think she could possibly be an heiress?

Looking back, she realized her gut had been shooting her warning signs for weeks, telling her she was getting in so deep, but she'd been too seduced by the idea of being a Sinclair she'd ignored them.

Who was she kidding? She believed her mother's story because she *wanted* to. All these years she'd wondered what it was she did to make her parents check out. She'd grasped at her mother's love affair because the truth hurt too much. Now truth wanted to make her pay by hammering itself home. *Mistake, mistake, mistake.*

The word repeated in her head as she played with the hem of her sweater set. Her *heiress costume,* she amended bitterly. "I should have known. I failed as an actress, as a daughter, as a mother…"

Steffi. What did she have to offer her daughter now? No inheritance. No father. She didn't even have her crappy job. All she had was this lousy apartment, a world filled with lowlifes like Wayne and a family history of drunken pickups. How long before her daughter started seeing her as the mistake she was, too?

Nausea rose in her throat. She rushed to the sink, making it seconds before losing her morning coffee. Heave after acidic heave burned her throat. Mike tried to rub small soothing circles on her back, but she shoved him away. To the other side of the room. Where she couldn't see the pity that had to be in his coppery eyes. Add him to her list of mistakes. He thought he'd made love to an heiress last night. Instead he got the premakeover Roxy. The one who couldn't measure up. Why would he want her now?

"It's over." She stared at the sink drain, watching the water wash away the mess. If only she could wash the fallout from this past month as easily.

"No. It's not over. Not yet."

He was pacing again, Roxy could hear his heels hitting the linoleum. "I'll go to Florida and interview your father myself. I should have in the first place. And your mother's medical records. We'll track them down. Maybe her doctor's still alive."

"Why? What's the use? Still going to be the same outcome."

"You don't know that."

Oh, but she did. "Face it, Mike, it's a lost cause."

"So, what? That's it? You're just going to quit?"

"What else am I supposed to do?

"You can keep fighting."

"Why? So I can make a bigger fool out of myself? Hope the Sinclairs give me some money to go away?"

"Why not? A lot better than hiding in your apartment playing the victim."

Playing the vict— Roxy whirled around. "What the hell is that supposed to mean?"

"Exactly what it sounds like."

"I am not playing anything." As if he would understand anyway. When had life ever kicked him in the teeth?

"Oh, no? Sure sounds it to me. One little phone call and you're ready to quit."

"As opposed to what? Fighting a lost cause so I can get bought off? That wasn't why I did this."

"Wasn't it?"

And so it came back to her being a fortune hunter. After all they'd shared. *After she gave him her heart.* Anger ripped through her. "You know it wasn't," she hissed. It took everything not to slap his face. "I wanted to know the truth."

"You're right. I'm sorry." The apology would carry more weight if she couldn't see the wheels turning in his head. Formulating the next line of attack.

It came with a milder voice. "All I meant was you came to me wanting to give Steffi a better life. You still can."

By basically coercing a payout. "I can't," she

told him. If she did lose her daughter's respect when she got older, she could at least keep some ability to look herself in the mirror.

Mike shook his head. "I can't let you quit. This case is way too important."

"Haven't you been listening? There is no case!"

"There has to be."

The ferocity with which he shouted the words shocked her. She knew he wasn't used to losing, but this… This was over-the-top. You'd think karma had played the joke on him instead of her. Surely she wasn't that important to him.

"Sorry," she told him. "Guess you'll have to win with another client."

"There is no other client."

What? She stared at him.

Mike ran a hand over his features. "I don't have any other clients," he repeated. "You're it."

"But, I don't understand. Your ad, the uptown offices…"

"Teetering on the brink of extinction." His fierceness turned sheepish. "You of all people should know things aren't always what they appear to be."

You'd think there'd be more clutter. Sophie's observation had been right. There was no clutter because there was no business.

Except for her. Her and her multimillion-dollar payday. A huge emptiness formed in the center of her chest. Roxy cut off his argument. She wasn't going to believe him anyway. No wonder he treated her like such an important client. Hanging around the bar. Doting on her.

Making love to her.

"That's all this was to you, wasn't it? A case. A way to salvage your business."

He started. Shock? Or guilt. "No. I mean, maybe things started out that way but…"

She didn't want to hear another argument. Here she thought last night meant something more, something deeper. That he felt the same emotions. But no, while she'd been making love, he'd been keeping his prized client happy.

Chalk up another bad choice.

For the first time since answering the door, she looked him straight in the eye.

"I think you should leave."

"Leave?" He looked genuinely surprised. "I'm not leaving you."

"Yeah, you are." He should be pleased. For once she wasn't the one walking away; she was making him do it. "What's that saying, fool me once, fool me twice? I'm not going to let you stick around so I can get fooled a third time."

Pushing her way past him, she marched to the

front door and flung it open. "Your job here is finished, Mr. Templeton."

Mike stared at her long and hard. "Don't do this, Roxy."

"Too late, I already have."

Took another couple of beats, but he finally got the message and walked away.

"Mommy?" From her place on the couch, Steffi broke the silence as soon as the door shut. "Mike didn't say goodbye."

Roxy kept her face to the wood, watching the lock swim in front of her eyes. "No, baby, he didn't."

Then again, she expected as much.

Damn, damn, damn!

The obscenity was the only word Mike was capable of forming. He chanted it the entire drive to his office, screaming it once or twice in the empty interior, hoping maybe, just maybe, he could make some sense of what happened in Roxy's apartment.

He had nothing.

Roxy couldn't be quitting. There was still plenty to fight. Until they had definitive, actual proof she had a case...

But no, she'd rather give up. Accept failure. He kicked over a potted plant. Dammit! Why did her father have to call this morning of all mornings?

Why couldn't the miserable bastard stay missing a little while longer?

Fine. If Roxy didn't want to pursue her claim, that was her business. He didn't need her or her case. He'd figure out another way to save his firm. He was a Templeton for crying out loud. He wasn't born to fail.

His toe kicked a scrap of cloth on the way to his desk. Bending down he found his tie from last night, tangled around the wheels of one of his guest chairs. Pain shot through him, starting deep in his stomach and exploding in vast emptiness across his chest. Letting out a groan, he squeezed the silk in his fist against the rising tide of memories. Images. Feelings. This was why you didn't get involved with clients. Because they made a man start believing in long-discarded emotions again. Made him think he was a winner again.

It's over. Roxy's words hit him hard. Did she know how much she ended with those two words? It was over.

He'd failed. His eyes dropped to the tie. In more ways than he thought possible.

"That's it? You left?"

"She told me to, Grant. What was I supposed to do? Fight her?"

From the disappointed looks his brother and Sophie were shooting him from across the living room, fight was exactly what they expected.

He bristled defensively. "I don't need a client who's going to fight me every step of the way."

Sophie folded her arms, jostling the Yorkshire terrier sleeping on her lap. "Referring to Roxanne as a client? Really?"

"She was a client. What should I call her?"

"I don't know. You tell me." Challenge glittered in her blue eyes.

Mike broke the stare. They didn't know he'd slept with Roxy. Some things were none of their business.

Besides, he was trying not to think about the night they spent together. Every time he did, his chest hurt.

"I feel bad for her," Grant said. "First her mother turns her world upside down, then her father turns it the other way. And on top of everything she loses her job?"

"Terrible," Sophie agreed. "Have you tried calling her?" she asked Mike.

Had he tried calling her? "I just finished saying the woman wants nothing to do with me."

"I know what you said. But have you called her?"

Damn her. She had a whiff of the truth and she wouldn't give up. "Half a dozen times," he replied, looking to his glass of Scotch. "She's blocked my number."

"Ouch. I'm sorry."

He shrugged, feigning indifference, hoping Sophie would drop the subject. "It is what it is. Can't be helped."

"You've got it bad, don't you?"

It was Grant, not Sophie. At his brother's question, Mike looked up. "What are you talking about?"

"You and your 'client'." He quoted the word with his fingers. "She's a lot more isn't she?"

"Don't be—" He stopped. What was the sense in protesting? They'd only keep hammering until he gave up the truth. Roxanne was more. A lot more. He could barely sit in his office without picturing her there with him. Laughing. Brushing the hair from her face. The other night, he actually drove himself to the Elderion, with some foolish notion that the lounge would dredge up older memories. Stupid. Nostalgia didn't have a chance against Roxanne. He didn't even make it to his regular table before her absence slammed into him like a truck and he had to go home.

"How'd you know?" he asked.

"Personal experience," his brother replied. "I've used the nonchalant act myself. Back before Sophie and I got our act together."

"I also told him how attentive you were the other weekend," Sophie added. "Unless you stare at all your clients like a lovesick puppy."

"No, just Roxanne." He took a drink. It had been a mistake, he wanted to add, but he couldn't. Nothing about Roxanne was a mistake. Not her history, not her annoying habit of overreacting and certainly not her. Grant and Sophie were right. He had it bad. Head over heels kind of bad.

"Doesn't matter," he said, moving to their fireplace. His chest was hurting again. He realized now the ache came from a place far deeper than his body. "She told me I didn't belong in her world."

"I'm not surprised," Grant replied.

"Gee, thanks."

"Seriously. No offense, but if I were her, you'd be the last person I'd want to see, too."

His brother appeared at his shoulder. "Here she is, feeling like the world kicked her in the teeth. A guy like you would only highlight the problems."

"What do you mean, a guy like me?"

"You know what I mean, Golden Boy. I'm sure she feels lousy enough about life without her polar opposite around to remind her how low she is."

"You're saying I made her feel inferior?"

"Not on purpose. But having grown up with you, I can say it's not always easy living with Mom and Dad's clone."

If only they knew....

He was more concerned with Roxanne right now. Had he really made her feel like less of a person? The thought made him sick. "I never meant to—"

No, you only insisted she have a makeover so she'd fit in better. Made her feel less than acceptable as she was.

He slapped his glass on the mantel. "God, I'm such a hypocrite."

"I wouldn't go that far," Grant said.

"I would. I have no right making anyone feel inadequate." He stared at his empty glass, how the diamonds on the cut crystal were perfectly uniformed except for one. "Especially now," he said in a quiet voice.

"What are you talking about?"

Taking a deep breath, Mike told them the whole story. About how the firm was failing and how the money from Roxanne's case was his last hope for keeping it afloat.

When he finished, Grant simply said, "Wow."

"I knew there wasn't enough paper clutter," Sophie said. "Green office, my foot."

"I'm surprised you didn't catch on sooner," Mike told her.

The relief he hoped he would feel upon confession didn't materialize. Instead all he felt was embarrassed for not saying anything sooner. Thinking of Roxanne having to share her story over and over, he developed new respect. Took real strength to raise a child on her own, no family, no real money. When he first met her, he'd recognized the mettle in her. If only she saw it herself. Maybe they'd still be talking.

"Do Mom and Dad know?" Grant was asking.

He shook his head. "Are you kidding? Like you said, I'm the Golden Boy. The one who's supposed to do everything right." The freakin' Templeton namesake. "I was giving them what they expected." Same way he always did.

"The curse of Templeton expectations rides again."

"Excuse me?" Looking to his brother, he saw the younger man had grown intensely interested in the label on his beer bottle. "The family emphasis on super success. Screwed us all up. I got a fear of success…you developed a fear of failure. Wonder what Nicole ended up with."

"Maybe she lucked out."

"Maybe." Grant pulled a strip off the label and rolled it between his fingers. "You do realize of course, that closing shop isn't the end of the world."

"For you, maybe. I'm the one who's supposed to be better than all the rest."

"That's why you pushed Roxanne's case so hard."

"I couldn't afford to have the case drag out for years in court." The tactic worked, he had to admit that. Just not the way he intended.

"The day she told me about her father, I was shocked. I…" Remembering that final conversation, he winced. "I focused more on the case than her."

"No wonder she threw you out."

"No wonder indeed."

"What are you going to do now?" Sophie asked.

"What do I do now?" He'd messed up his career and his relationship with Roxanne. Failure wasn't a place he was used to operating from. He was lost.

"You could try talking with her," Sophie said.

"I told you, I already have. She wants nothing to do with me."

A hand clapped on his shoulder. Grant. "If you want, I can share with you a valuable piece of advice I got last summer. Something you said to me in fact."

Valuable advice? From him? "I have to hear this pearl of wisdom. What is it?"

"When's the last time a Templeton didn't go after what he wanted?"

CHAPTER THIRTEEN

"Look, Mommy. The animals made a merry-go-round!"

Roxy drew her attention away from the message on her cell phone only to wince at the plastic toys arranged in a circle on the living room floor. "That's nice. Are they having fun?"

"Uh-huh. I liked the merry-go-round we went to. Can we go back there?"

"What's wrong with the one in Central Park?"

Steffi looked up from making the horses dance. "This one has the rabbit," she said matter-of-factly.

"Oh."

"So can we go?"

Go to Bryant Park. Took her twenty-nine years to get to the place, and now it would be forever tainted with memories.

"We'll see," she said to Steffi. She hated saying no outright when she had no logical reason to give the four-year-old. What was she supposed to say? No, baby, I can't because thinking about the carousel makes Mommy cry? "Maybe someday."

"Okay. Can Mike come?"

A knife twisted in her chest. "I don't think we'll see Mike anymore."

"Why not?"

"Because we're not working together anymore. We're all done with our business."

"Why?"

Roxy sighed. Because Grandma's big deathbed confession turned out to be a deathbed fantasy, and then Mommy and Mike said some hurtful things to each other and Mommy sent Mike away, but that's okay because he would have left eventually anyway and she wanted to keep her heart from breaking. Except she didn't move fast enough and her heart ached anyway.

How was she supposed to explain that to a four-year-old?

As luck would have it, she didn't have to because someone knocked on the door. "I don't want to go see Mrs. Ortega," Steffi immediately started whining.

"We aren't going to Mrs. Ortega's," Roxy told her. "It's probably Priti from next door looking to borrow something."

But it wasn't Priti. It was Wayne. His shoulder rubbed against her as he pushed his way in.

"We got any beer left?" he asked, strolling to the kitchen.

"We don't have anything," she replied sharply. "Alexis's not here. She's out with PJ." PJ, along with Wayne, had become a fixture in the apartment this week, meaning she now had two freeloaders living there. And annoying as that was, Roxy couldn't say a blessed thing. A little fact Alexis took great pleasure in. Along with all the other misfortunes that had befallen Steffi.

He came back into view, a can in each hand. "I hate cans," he said. "We gotta get more bottles."

Tell it to someone who cares. "I told you, Alexis isn't here. Wait a moment. How'd you get in the building anyway?"

"I had some business to take care of."

Business. She could imagine. "Well, you don't have any business here, so why don't you take off?"

"Relax." Wayne held up his arms. "I'm not here to cause trouble. I came by to see you. Thought maybe you might need some company."

The idea repulsed her beyond repulsion. "No, thanks. Steffi and I are fine by ourselves."

"Now don't go being like that. I know your lawyer man up and dumped you cause you ain't getting money."

"Mike didn't dump me." If anything, she dumped

him, not that Wayne would believe her. "There was nothing to dump since we weren't having that kind of relationship."

"What kind of relationship is that?" Wayne suddenly appeared next to her shoulder, his breath sour from beer.

"Professional." Why was she even entertaining the guy's questions? Oh, right, because of Alexis. That reason was starting to wear thin.

Wayne smiled. "I can do professional," he said in a low voice that was supposed to sound sexy. "I can do anything you want. Like I told you. I treat my women real good. What do you say?" To illustrate his point, he ran an index finger down her arm. Roxy choked back the bile in her throat. Instead she looked over at Steffi, who was watching the entire exchange with her eyes as wide as saucers. "Steffi, baby, how about you take Dusty and go down to your room and play for a few minutes?"

As if hearing his name made her worry something would happen, the little girl grabbed her purple-and-white friend. "What about the merry-go-round?" she asked.

"Let's give the animals a break and I'll bring them in a few minutes, okay? Now please be a good girl and go to your room."

"Yeah, kid," Wayne echoed, winking in Roxy's direction. "Beat it."

The little girl rose to her feet, but wavered. Roxy gave her a nod and a smile to let her know everything would be all right. It worked, and eventually the child toddled to her bedroom and shut the door.

Roxy waited until she heard the click before whirling around and slapping Wayne's hand away. "Don't you ever talk to me or my daughter like that again, do you hear?"

The nineteen-year-old responded with a click of his piercing against his teeth. "Alexis ain't going to like you talking to me that way."

That was it. This blight of a human being had been darkening her doorstep long enough. Suggesting she would sleep with him because she hit hard times? She may have sunk low, but she would never sink that low. Ever.

She jabbed her index finger into his shoulder. "Look here, you little wannabe punk, I don't care whose baby brother you are. You so much as look at me or my little girl, and I will squeeze your private parts so hard you'll be singing soprano. Do you understand? Not one single look. Now take your beer and get out of my apartment."

Alexis would definitely not like this, but frankly she didn't care. There was only so much a woman should put up with.

Openly ignoring her threat, Wayne looked her

up and down. "What if I don't want to leave?" he asked, stepping closer.

Roxy grabbed her cell phone, which thankfully, she still had in her pocket. "Then I'll call the police," she told him. "We'll see how your parole officer feels about you getting arrested. Especially since you were doing business." She pushed the first button. "Nine."

"Alexis's going to be ticked."

"I don't care. The only reason I'm giving you a countdown at all is because of Alexis." If she had actual proof of his "business," she wouldn't even give him that courtesy. She'd have his skinny butt hauled back to prison in a second. "One," she said.

"All right, all right," he said before she could repeat the last number. "Don't get all wigged out."

"You don't know wigged out, pal. Now get out."

"Uppity..." He muttered the second word but Roxy could guess it. The same oath he used before. This time he curled his lip in distaste.

"You think you're so much better than us because you did a few TV interviews and some dude bought you some fancy clothes," he said, "but I got news for you. You ain't all that."

"Maybe not," Roxy replied. "But I'm still better than you."

And she was better than this life.

* * *

"I don't like Wayne," Steffi told her when Roxy tucked her in bed a little while later. "He's mean."

Out of the mouths of babes... Roxy smoothed the sheets around her chest. "I think he is, too, but don't you worry. I won't let him bother you anymore."

"Is that why we're hiding in the bedroom? Because he's mean?"

"We're in the bedroom," Roxy said, "because it's bedtime." And yes, because she was afraid he might decide to come back, and the bedroom door had workable locks. "We can have a slumber party."

"Like the ponies?"

"Exactly."

Steffi snuggled in against her pillow, a little red-haired angel. She was a great kid, yet untouched by the Waynes in this world. So far, Roxy'd been able to keep them at bay. She intended to keep doing so. Tomorrow morning, she'd start looking for a new job and a new apartment. Maybe some place out of the city, where Steffi could have a yard. After all, when she started this Sinclair heiress business, hadn't it been to give her daughter a better life? If Wayne's little visit did anything, it told her she could sit around licking her wounds, mourning the losses she'd never get back or she could get off her duff and give her daughter the life she deserved. She chose the latter.

"I like Mike better," Steffi said, her eyes starting to blink with sleep. "He's nicer."

Speaking of losses she'd never get back. "Yes, he is. He's very nice."

"Do you like him?"

She a lot more than liked him. When he walked out, he took her heart with him. "It's complicated, baby."

"Complicated means hard. Mike told me."

"Mike's right."

"He said the same thing when I asked if he liked you."

Smart guy, thought Roxy. Notice he didn't come straight out and say yes, either.

"I don't think it is."

"What is?" She missed what her daughter was trying to say.

Steffi yawned. "Hard. Unless the person doesn't like you back. But you and Mike like each other so—" she yawned again "—I don't think it's hard."

Roxy didn't know how to respond to that. How could she explain to a four-year-old that feelings weren't so black and white? There were other issues that made relationships complicated, such as being able to look the man she loved in the eye. Or look at herself.

"I love you, Mommy," Steffi said.

Heart overflowing, Roxy kissed her forehead. "I love you, too. Sweet dreams."

Giving her one last kiss, she turned out the light and laid down on her bed. For the first time since talking to her father, she felt a surge of positivity. Standing up to Wayne made her feel stronger. In control. A little bit like...

Like she had when she was doing the interviews.

At the time, she said she felt like a different person was giving those interviews. Some woman she didn't know. Capable. Confident.

Could it be that woman was still there? She certainly showed up to tell off Wayne.

Better than staying in your apartment playing victim. Mike's words came back. She'd been hurt and angry when he said them, and retaliated in kind. But now she wondered. Did she have a choice?

"Mommy?" Steffi's voice reached out through the darkness. She hoped the little girl was simply restless, and not stressed out about Wayne or other problems.

"Yes, baby?"

"I hope liking Mike stops being hard. So you won't be so sad."

Roxy felt the ache before it had fully formed. The slow winding pang of loss. "That'd be nice."

"Maybe if we took him to the merry-go-round, you could like him again. You smiled a lot that day."

"Yes, I did." How could she not? It'd been a magical day.

"Mike smiled a lot, too. We should go to the merry-go-round again." Having voiced her decision, she gave a satisfied sigh. Roxy heard the rustle of sheets and, a few seconds later, the slow, steady sound of breathing.

Could it really be so simple? Were all these obstacles things she made up? Put in her own way? Mike accused her of playing the victim. That's certainly what she'd been doing these past couple days.

She rolled on her side. In some ways, that's what her mother did, too. She clung to her love for Wentworth so strongly, she faded away from everyone else. At least Wentworth was willing to act and make something happen. He died planning to take a stand against his father. In his mind, loving someone wasn't so complicated.

Okay, she thought folding her arms behind her head. Maybe she wasn't a Sinclair by blood. Didn't mean she couldn't steal a little of Wentworth's determination.

Without thinking, she reached for her cell phone that lay on the nightstand. Mike's text was still on the screen, undeleted, waiting for her. *You were not a mistake,* he'd written. Her case? Her? Both? The words, coupled with her newfound control couldn't help but give her hope.

When did a Templeton not go after what he wanted?

Mike remembered all too well when he posted the same question to his brother. Circumstances were different. Grant and Sophie were simply being proud and stubborn. All they needed was for one of them to make the first move. In his case, he'd tried to talk to Roxanne, and she refused.

Who could blame her? She'd been hurting and he was worried about what? A law practice? Letting down his family?

Wentworth Sinclair would be ashamed.

He slapped a file in the large cardboard box. The downside of being a small law practice was that when it came time to move, you had to do the actual moving. There were no administrative staff members or clerks to help you out.

Just as well, thought Mike as he assembled another file storage box. He wasn't fit for the company of others anyway.

Wentworth's letters lay in a stack nearby. He

ran his finger over the black scrawl. Six times. Six times he'd called and not so much as a voice mail. In the end, he settled for sending her a text message, hoping the apology would help.

"So it's true."

Judge Michael Templeton, Jr. wore a Burberry trench coat and his salt-and-pepper hair was combed back, emphasizing his handsome, time-sharpened features. He entered the room as though the office was his own and sat down, opting for Mike's desk chair over one of the guest seats. "When Jim Brassard told me you inquired about a position, I thought for sure he misunderstood. What's going on?"

Mike dropped another file in the box. "Isn't it obvious?" he said. "I'm closing up shop."

"I meant why are you closing your practice? You didn't mention anything. I thought you enjoyed being your own boss."

"I also enjoy eating."

Based on the way he stiffened, his father didn't appreciate the sharp comeback. "Is that your way of saying business is a little slow?"

Mike chuckled at his father's adjective. "A little," he replied. "You may not have noticed, but we're in an economic downturn."

"If business is slow, then get out there and double your efforts. Beat the bushes for business. You don't throw in the towel, Michael. That's not how we do things."

How we do things. The phrase set Mike's teeth on edge. God, but he was so tired of hearing how "they" were raised. How he was supposed to be.

"Do you remember when you first started swimming and you couldn't keep up with the rest of your squad?" his father asked.

"What I remember is being two years younger." His father convinced the coach he needed the challenge.

"Exactly. But you dug in and by the end of the year you were beating those boys."

Of course he dug in. He was eight years old and his father was dragging him to a swimming pool every weekend for extra practice. Pushing him every step of the way till his times improved. And Mike obeyed. To win his approval. To make his father proud. On and on the cycle went. Go higher. Be better. Be the best. So many expectations, his shoulders hurt.

"We didn't raise you to be a quitter, Michael. When I was your age, I already had a thriving practice with two associates. Did I have tough times, sure, but I worked for my success. I thought we raised you the same way."

Oh, they did, all right. His father raised him to

be a mirror image. The perfect namesake. "What if I don't want it?" he asked aloud.

"What are you talking about? Of course you want it. We talked about this last year. How you'd done all you could at Ashby Gannon, and should be stepping out on your own."

We discussed. *You should.* Not once did they discuss what Mike wanted. God, wasn't it time he stopped being a puppet and grew up?

"People change their minds," he told his father. "Maybe I don't want this—" he waved his arm around the room "—anymore. Maybe I want something else."

"You've wanted to be a lawyer since you were eight years old, Michael."

"Did I? Because I remember at eight years old I wanted to be a pirate." He slapped the file he was holding on the table. "In fact, that's the last time I remember wanting anything that wasn't shaped or picked for me." Until six nights ago, with Roxanne. Holding her was all his idea. Best one he'd ever had, too. "The only reason I said I wanted to be a lawyer was because that's what you were, and like any eight-year-old, I wanted to be like my father. I had no idea you would decide 'like' meant mirror image."

His father scoffed. "I did no such thing."

"Didn't you? Swimming. The debate club. Your

alma maters. What was all that about then, if not to repeat your past glories?"

"To help you be the best you could be. For heaven's sake, Michael, you make it sound like we put a gun to your head."

"No gun, just a whole lot of expectations."

"If you're saying we pushed you, yes. We wanted the best for you."

"You didn't want the best." Roxanne wanted the best. She was willing to do anything, including the one thing she feared the most—losing her daughter's respect to give Steffi a better life. "You wanted us to *be* the best. Always. Because God forbid we reflect badly on the family."

"That is not true!" his father bellowed, an uncharacteristic tone of voice for him and a sign Mike had hit a nerve dead-on. He pushed further.

"If so, then why are you here?"

"Because Jim Brassard told me—"

"Told you I was closing up shop and you were afraid he was telling the truth. Well, guess what, he was. I failed. I opened my own law practice, crashed and burned. Deal with it."

Soon as Mike said the words, a thousand pounds lifted from his shoulders. He'd done it. He'd failed and the world didn't end.

Not that you could tell from the look on his father's face. Disappointment marked every line.

"Fine," the elder Templeton said. "You're closing your firm, and it's my fault. Happy?"

Mike shook his head. His father truly didn't understand, did he? None of this was about him. Took Mike till just this moment to realize his succeeding or failing was all his. Same with the choices he made. "Why does it have to involve you at all, Dad? Sometimes bad luck happens."

He could tell his father wasn't convinced. Maybe never would be. For the first time, Mike realized there was nothing he could do about what his father thought. "So what do you plan to do? Go back to Ashby Gannon or Brassard's firm?"

"Maybe. I don't know." The uncertainty had a liberating feel. Suddenly the world was wide-open.

There was one thing he did want. Or rather, two. Question was, did they want him?

Only one way to know for sure. Forgetting all about his father and packing, Mike grabbed the stack of letters off his desk. Wentworth would be proud.

"Where are you going?" his father called after him.

"What a Templeton's supposed to do," he replied, grinning. More for himself and the world than to the man seated at his desk.

"I'm going after what I want."

* * *

First thing he'd do when he got to Roxanne's would be to apologize and ask for another chance. She'd have to talk with him eventually, right? If necessary, he'd camp out in her hallway and accost her when she stepped outside. Whatever he needed to do.

He made it as far as the lobby before his mind started playing tricks on him. Getting off the elevator he swore he saw Steffi coming through the revolving door.

"Mike!" The figment waved brightly. "Look, Mommy, it's Mike."

His wishful eyes traveled to the woman behind her. It really was Roxanne. Dressed in a pair of faded jeans and the pale blue turtleneck, she'd never looked lovelier. When she saw him, she offered a tremulous smile.

Mike's pulse skipped a couple beats. He stopped dead. "Hey!" he said.

Silence filled the gap as he struggled with what to say next, hindered by the Manhattan-size lump lodged in his throat. "I was on my way to your apartment," he finally managed to say.

"You were? Why?"

To kiss you senseless. "To return your mother's letters," he said. As if it would prove his point, he held up his briefcase.

"Oh," she replied.

Was that disappointment he caught flickering across her face? He was afraid to hope. "Why are you…?"

"Same thing."

"Oh." His heart dropped. Guess it wasn't disappointment after all.

"Where's your tie?" Steffi asked.

"My what? Oh, my tie." Automatically his hand went to the collar of his T-shirt. "I didn't wear one today. I didn't want it to get dirty while I was packing."

Roxanne frowned, hearing his answer. "Packing?" she asked. "Are you going somewhere?"

"Eventually. I hope. I'm closing my practice."

"Why?" Perhaps she didn't realize, but she rushed toward him a few steps. "Is something—? Did something—?"

Mike saved her the trouble of searching for the right question and explained. When he finished, she looked down at her shoes. "The money from my case. You needed it to stay afloat."

He always said she was quick. "I needed the case for a lot of reasons," he told her. "Notoriety, money."

"Then if I hadn't…"

"You aren't to blame for anything." He refused to pile on guilt when she had enough issues on her shoulders. "This was my doing, one hundred percent. I took the case for all the wrong reasons. That's why, when you dropped the lawsuit, I acted like such a jerk."

"You were worried."

"Not worried. Afraid." Taking a deep breath, he said aloud the truth he'd kept to himself for a long time. "I was afraid of what would happen when I failed."

"Because you never had a choice," she said quietly.

"Exactly." She understood. "I thought I'd be letting everybody down."

"And now?"

"Now I'm thinking the only person I've failed all these years is myself. Plus you."

She shook her head. "You never failed me."

He didn't? Giving in to his longing to be closer, he stepped forward, hoping when he drew near, she wouldn't back away. "I've been taking a good long look at how I see success," he said. He thought about his father, still upstairs. "Some of it in the past few minutes in fact."

"What did you decide?"

"That I need to reexamine my personal definition of success and failure. See, I've spent a good portion of my life chasing one and fearing the other. Turns out I never really knew either till I met this woman who managed to be both sweet and graceful at the same time, in spite of all the stuff life tossed her."

Of course, she'd argue that she's not very successful at all.

"That so?"

"Uh-huh." He lucked out. She didn't back away. He continued closing the gap. "In fact," he said, "she'd argue she's a complete failure, even though that couldn't be further from the truth.

"She's very feisty," he said with a smile. "Before you showed up, I was debating about going to her apartment and camping out on her doorstep till she spoke to me."

"You were going to sleep on the steps?" Steffi asked. "Do you have a sleeping bag?"

Leave it to a four-year-old to ask the important questions. "I was hoping it wouldn't come to that, but if your mother wouldn't talk to me, I would have."

"Mommy's the woman?"

Mike nodded.

"But we came here because Mommy wanted to talk to you."

He wasn't sure if he should let the hope that lodged in his chest grow or not. He decided to take a chance. "What did you want to talk with me about?"

* * *

Roxy blinked back her tears. She'd rehearsed this scene in her head a dozen times last night, but none of her versions involved Mike saying such beautiful things or his looking so breathtakingly casual. She spent all night arguing back and forth with herself over coming here. Did she take a chance and trust the sincerity that always glowed in his eyes or did she give up like her mother?

"Did you mean it?" she asked him. "What you said in your text?"

He nodded. "Every word. You were definitely not a mistake."

Relief whooshed from her lungs. Five words. Six if you added the new word, definitely. Five words that meant everything. She felt them wrap around her heart, unlocking the feelings inside and telling her that yes, this choice was worth making.

"Funny, but I had to do some reevaluating, too," she told him. "Seems this guy I know told me I was playing victim, letting all the 'stuff' life threw me convince me I'm not worthy of anything better."

"He was wrong."

"Wait!" She touched her fingers to his lips. "He was right. I was crying 'poor me,' but not anymore."

"What made you change your mind?"

She smiled, thinking of the letters in his briefcase. "My mother. I didn't want to be like her. I didn't want to find myself lying on my death-bed pining for the man I couldn't have. Especially when I had the power to get him back."

Strong arms wrapped around her waist, drawing her close. "You never lost him," he whispered.

Roxy's heart soared. "I'm so very glad," she whispered back. Rising on tiptoes, she brought her mouth to his. "I have a question. What would you have done if the successful woman didn't listen to you?"

"I would have looked her in the eye and told her I was grateful for every second I knew her. That nothing we shared was a mistake."

His words reached deep into her soul, healing its wounds. Telling her she'd made the right choice.

"And then," he said, fingers tangling in her hair, "I would have kissed her till she realized I'm crazy about her. I have been since the minute she stormed out of my office in a huff."

"Sounds perfect," Roxy whispered, her voice catching on the tears. "Because I'm pretty sure she's crazy about you, too."

In the end, it wasn't the words that convinced her, but the emotion that glowed from his eyes while he spoke. Looking deep into them, she saw love, compassion and the coppery-brown sincerity that captured her heart. For the first time, seeing them mixed together didn't frighten her, either. If anything, they made her feel more successful than she'd ever felt in her life. Because she loved and was loved.

"Just in case, though…" She touched his cheek. "You should probably kiss her senseless anyway."

"My pleasure," Mike replied. Slipping an arm around her waist, he pulled her close, his lips speaking a truth all their own. Only a small tug on her sweater stopped the moment.

"Does this mean Mike's going to come with us to the merry-go-round?" Steffi asked.

Mike laughed and scooped the little girl into his arms. "Absolutely, my little pony! There is nothing I want to do more right now." He smiled at Roxy over the little girl's head.

And Roxy, smiling back, believed every word.

* * * * *

LARGER-PRINT BOOKS!

GET 2 FREE LARGER-PRINT NOVELS PLUS
2 FREE GIFTS!

HARLEQUIN®

Romance

From the Heart, For the Heart

YES! Please send me 2 FREE LARGER-PRINT Harlequin® Romance novels and my 2 FREE gifts (gifts are worth about $10). After receiving them, if I don't wish to receive any more books, I can return the shipping statement marked "cancel." If I don't cancel, I will receive 6 brand-new novels every month and be billed just $4.59 per book in the U.S. or $5.24 per book in Canada. That's a savings of at least 20% off the cover price! It's quite a bargain! Shipping and handling is just 50¢ per book in the U.S. and 75¢ per book in Canada.* I understand that accepting the 2 free books and gifts places me under no obligation to buy anything. I can always return a shipment and cancel at any time. Even if I never buy another book, the two free books and gifts are mine to keep forever.

119/319 HDN FVSK

Name _____ (PLEASE PRINT) _____

Address _____ Apt. # _____

City _____ State/Prov. _____ Zip/Postal Code _____

Signature (if under 18, a parent or guardian must sign) _____

Mail to the Harlequin® Reader Service:
IN U.S.A.: P.O. Box 1867, Buffalo, NY 14240-1867
IN CANADA: P.O. Box 609, Fort Erie, Ontario L2A 5X3
Are you a current subscriber to Harlequin Romance books and want to receive the larger-print edition?
Call 1-800-873-8635 or visit www.ReaderService.com.

* Terms and prices subject to change without notice. Prices do not include applicable taxes. Sales tax applicable in N.Y. Canadian residents will be charged applicable taxes. Offer not valid in Quebec. This offer is limited to one order per household. Not valid for current subscribers to Harlequin Romance Larger-Print books. All orders subject to credit approval. Credit or debit balances in a customer's account(s) may be offset by any other outstanding balance owed by or to the customer. Please allow 4 to 6 weeks for delivery. Offer available while quantities last.

Your Privacy—The Harlequin® Reader Service is committed to protecting your privacy. Our Privacy Policy is available online at www.ReaderService.com or upon request from the Harlequin Reader Service.

We make a portion of our mailing list available to reputable third parties that offer products we believe may interest you. If you prefer that we not exchange your name with third parties, or if you wish to clarify or modify your communication preferences, please visit us at www.ReaderService.com/consumerchoice or write to us at Harlequin Reader Service Preference Service, P.O. Box 9062, Buffalo, NY 14269. Include your complete name and address.

HRLP13

The series you love are now available in

LARGER PRINT!

The books are complete and unabridged—
printed in a larger type size to make it
easier on your eyes.

HARLEQUIN

Romance

From the Heart, For the Heart

HARLEQUIN

MEDICAL™

Pulse-racing romance,
heart-racing medical drama

HARLEQUIN

INTRIGUE®

BREATHTAKING ROMANTIC SUSPENSE

HARLEQUIN

Presents®

Seduction and Passion Guaranteed!

HARLEQUIN

super romance®

Exciting, emotional, unexpected!

Try **LARGER PRINT** today!

Visit: www.ReaderService.com
Call: 1-800-873-8635

H HARLEQUIN®

A *Romance* FOR EVERY MOOD™

www.ReaderService.com

HLPDIR13

ReaderService.com

Manage your account online!

- Review your order history
- Manage your payments
- Update your address

We've designed the Harlequin® Reader Service website just for you.

Enjoy all the features!

- Reader excerpts from any series
- Respond to mailings and special monthly offers
- Discover new series available to you
- Browse the Bonus Bucks catalog
- Share your feedback

Visit us at:

ReaderService.com

RS13